Ring of Fire

I0671874

Benchland Book Three

An action story spanning a half century

**A war story from a time when villages were often
devastated by barbarian raiders**

**A story of advancing technology . . .
of ancient earth-centered spirituality . . .
and of love and community in a society led by
women of wisdom**

The **Benchland** is a shelf of fertile ground high on the wall of a river canyon in the Scandinavian north, accessible only through a large cave. Safe from raids and sheltered in winter, Benchland and cave were settled 5,000 years ago by a small group that grew to a thriving colony. A huge trove of paintings on the cave walls, a pictorial history of the colony, is now a historic and archaeological treasure.

The three-volume Benchland Series immerses the reader in life late in the Age of Copper. *Ring of Fire's* characters and setting will be familiar to readers of the first two Benchland books, but it can be read independently.

The conclusion of the Benchland Saga

Ring of Fire

Books by Jay Hosler and Peggy Harrison

Norm and Burny: The Black Square

The Girl with the Gold Coin: Norm and Burny Book Two

Rockslide: Journals from the Age of Copper

Spirit Chamber: Tales from the Benchland

Benchland Book Three

RING OF FIRE

Jay Hosler and Peggy Harrison

Ring of Fire is a work of fiction. Its characters, events, and places are either the product of the authors' imagination or are used fictionally. Any resemblance to actual events or places, or to persons living or dead, is entirely coincidental.

Printed in the United States of America

ISBN-13 978-0692743294
ISBN-10: 0692743294

Published by Benchland Publishing
admin@benchlandpubs.com

First edition

This book is dedicated to

Our Readers

who gave their time to make it what it is

during the beta reading event of May, 2016

Punish her he must,
For a breach of his own iron law
Would topple all he had made,
Bring the world low.

Yet Brynhild, youngest, most valiant, best loved,
He could not abandon, even in his wrath.
Odin wreathed her with protection,
A ward against evil descending as she slept,
A ring of fire.

—The Lesser Edda

Contents

Part One

Warriors

Mist. No—smoke. Then flame. The village burning. Men shouting. Terrified women and children screaming. Death everywhere.

I am shaking in panic, afraid we will all die. Crying in pain. I am bound.

Then relief. Running free. Not alone.

In safety I am flooded by the feeling of a spirit—the spirit of a place that will shelter me.

Amma wept as she told me no little girl should have such a dream of her future.

Eight years before *Rockslide* . . .

1

HE WAS OUT COLLECTING FIREWOOD by dawn as usual. He wore his heavy cloak, for mornings were still cold even now that the snow was mostly gone, and the family would need a fire until midday.

Often he met other boys with their slings and baskets in the woods nearest the village, but it was nearly stripped of firewood now, and he was alone in the large forest farther upstream. He quickly picked up a full load from the wealth of storm-blown spruce branches. The green of the forest was vivid against heavy grey clouds, and the breeze had died away. Sigurd sensed an approaching storm, perhaps even a late snowstorm.

Afterward he realized that going to the farther forest had saved his life.

BEFORE STARTING FOR HOME, he sat on a fallen log beside the stream, at the edge of a large frost-covered meadow. The village looked small in the distance, lying between two hills at the stream canyon's narrow mouth. Elvdal was its name—twelve houses west of the stream, which hugged the eastern hill as it left the canyon to flow out over the flats toward the river. The western hill hid his own house, which was far enough from the stream to be inconvenient, for Sigurd's chores included fetching water in hide bags. Smoke would be curling above the house; his mother had already started the fire when he left. His brother would be milking the goats, his little sister helping with breakfast.

Sigurd was the middle child, at thirteen a sturdy boy, as big as his mother, not as tall as Leif, his older brother, but already heavier. Sigurd was the family expert with bow and arrow, best of all the boys in the village, and a fine hunter. He never left home without his bow and arrows, even on wood-gathering trips.

Sigurd's father had been ill for two years and bedridden since midwinter. He had hoped to recover as the weather improved, but his cough was worse now than a month ago, and he was weaker. Sigurd feared the outcome, and every morning as he gathered wood he spoke prayers to the forest spirits for his father's recovery.

After the prayers, he sat quietly in the stillness.

Raising his head at a distant noise, he was startled to see a plume of dark smoke above the hidden western part of the village. He jumped anxiously to his feet, shouldered his load of firewood, and started downstream toward home, hurrying as much as possible considering the weight of wood on his back. The path dropped steeply, and he soon lost sight of the village. He passed through the lower forest at a trot and had nearly reached the fields upstream from the village when he heard screaming. He rushed forward to where he could see what was happening.

The village was in flames. Gangs of armed warriors ran from house to house setting fires and killing any who emerged. Every house was burning, the flames roaring, merging above the village into a tower of black smoke.

Sigurd knew his family was dead or dying. His father, brother, sister. His mother.

He saw at least fifty attackers, more than enough to overwhelm the village even if there had been warning. The screams of women mixed with battle shouts as men sought to defend themselves, but they were too few and were struck down, every one.

Sigurd could not possibly change the outcome.

The scene felt unreal to him, and he stood numb. Fifty armed men had burned a village and killed nearly a hundred people too quickly for him to comprehend, his conscious self crushed between the enormity of the act and its impossible quickness.

"S IGURD!"

He turned to see a younger village boy looking dumbly at the slaughter.

"Gunnar." The sound of Sigurd's own voice surprised him; he had thought he would never speak again. "You don't have your bow and arrows?"

"We should hide. Or they'll kill us too."

"They won't come here. They came down the river from the west. I first saw fire from the upper forest. It was behind the western hill. They'll continue downriver toward the sea." Already the attackers were gathering downstream from the village, herding dozens of goats, sheep, and pigs, the village's chief wealth. The boys could see the men and animals clearly.

Gunnar stood sobbing. A cold rain spattered about the two boys. Sigurd felt a sick despair but knew that yielding to it would change nothing, that in the time it usually took him to eat breakfast, the world had turned completely around to face into darkness and horror. He knew in his bones that he would need all his wits and energy simply to stay alive. Grief would have to wait.

S IGURD HAD HEARD ALL HIS LIFE of the Raiders from the North, who ransacked and burned and killed without mercy, but those stories were old ones. He remembered both his grandmothers, who told terrible tales from their youth, although always finishing with how the raiders had been beaten back and thirty peaceful years had passed. His grandparents feared raiders would return. His mother and father hoped otherwise.

Sigurd and Gunnar spent the rest of the day and all that night huddled in the forest, in the rain, without fire or food. The marauders camped downstream from the village with a huge bonfire and in the morning walked off eastward toward the sea. The boys entered the village then—together, so that neither would face alone what they knew they would find.

The rain had stopped, but the day was much colder. Everything was soaked, and the village smelled of sodden ashes and death. Bodies lay everywhere, many of them badly burned. Many houses had been reduced to ash, burning quickly as flaming pieces of thatch roof fell in. Of Gunnar's house the boys found only remnants, and in the ash and burned rubble they found no trace of Gunnar's family. At Sigurd's house the posts were still standing. The charred body of Sigurd's father lay where his bed had been. Sigurd found a small body outside the house; turning it over, he recognized his sister. He searched the area for his mother and brother, but to no avail.

He carried his sister to the forest, where the boys had spent the night, and then returned for his father. On that trip he found a stone shovel blade and carried it back to dig a grave. He laid the two bodies side by side and covered them. Gunnar helped with the digging and sobbed quietly as Sigurd spoke the prayers for the dead.

"I WISH I HAD DIED TOO," Gunnar said. He and Sigurd sat at their fire. It was nearly dark. They had set out hunting in the early afternoon, but when he realized Gunnar was a liability, Sigurd asked him to build and tend a fire instead. The hunt dragged on all afternoon, and Sigurd was lucky to return with a poor thin winter rabbit. Gunnar had made a foraging trip to the village by himself and returned with fire tools, a knife blade from which the handle had burned away, and an undamaged bone-handled flint hunting knife.

The boys ate every morsel of rabbit, their only food in two days.

"Do not speak those wishes," Sigurd said. "Do not think them. We were chosen to live, and we must abide by that." Even as he said the words he knew their falseness, that given the choice, he too would rather have died than face life without his family. That night as he lay awake trying to come to terms with his loss, he planned the following morning's hunt and wondered whether he was strong enough and skilled enough to live on his own, especially providing for a younger boy.

2

LIFE IS SIMPLE at the level of the essentials. Find a way to stay warm—or die of cold. Find food—or starve. The nights were cruel even in good weather, and that spring was a time of unrelenting cold rain. Sigurd dreamed of killing a deer some early morning or late evening, but the does were wary and the bucks scarce, and he was lucky to take enough rabbits to survive.

Sigurd and Gunnar hiked upstream, heading for a smaller village several days' walk away in a different watershed, over a mountain pass. Sigurd was unwilling to share the flat river plain with the raiders. It grew colder as the boys climbed, and by the third day their path was covered with snow. Their hide shoes soaked through, and Sigurd built a fire under an overhanging rock face to dry them.

The boys were warm and dry by the time they slept that night, but they awoke to shrieking wind and long before morning were in the midst of a spring blizzard.

"This can't last long, at this time of year," Sigurd said.

Gunnar did not respond. He was a slighter child than Sigurd and cold through. Their overhanging rock protected them from much of the wind and snow, but when Sigurd tried to rekindle the fire, the wind defeated him. The two boys huddled together for warmth and did not sleep the rest of the night.

BY FIRST LIGHT the storm slackened to occasional flurries, but the snow on the ground was deeper than the day before. Heavy overcast hid the sun, and the day was icy cold. As Sigurd built a fire and prepared to set out hunting, he was anxious about Gunnar, who was lethargic and pale after going without food for a full day.

They had camped well above the stream and the river of cold air that follows it. Sigurd approached the stream cautiously to avoid spooking any game there and saw the doe at the moment she sensed him. She whipped her head toward him, ears up, looking for motion. Sigurd froze. By the time the doe convinced herself that she was not threatened and resumed browsing, Sigurd was numb with cold, barely able to move. He decided to try a difficult shot rather than risk scaring the deer away by going closer. He edged silently behind a tree and pumped his arms to dispel the numbness in his hands. Still out of the deer's sight, he notched an arrow and drew the bow. Then, ever so slowly, he stepped out from behind the tree.

The doe was looking intently downstream. She exploded into motion as a screaming child ran into view with two wolves in grim pursuit, closing fast. Sigurd turned toward the boy, who was stumbling in panic. Sigurd guessed he was about six.

"Over here!"

As the boy looked up, the lead wolf sprang. Sigurd's arrow struck him in the chest, and he crumpled in mid-leap. Sigurd notched another arrow and turned to face the second wolf, but the pursuit was over. The boy leapt behind Sigurd, and the second wolf veered off and ran. The fallen wolf lay still, dying.

"Are you hurt?"

The boy shook his head.

"Are you alone?"

Another shake of the head. "My mother . . . I was ahead, and the wolves chased me. I thought they would catch me."

"Your mother is here?"

The boy pointed back along the path. As Sigurd looked that way, a woman appeared, panting as she ran up the stream with her heavy pack.

The boy ran to her. "Mama, the wolves wanted to kill me, but he shot one and saved me."

The mother's relief came out as an angry outburst. "Ragni, I *told* you to stay close. Don't you *ever—*"

She broke off and looked at Sigurd. "You're only a boy yourself. What are you *doing* here?"

Sigurd drew a deep breath and told the story in a rush. "I am Sigurd, and I'm not only a boy. I'll be fourteen at midsummer. I came from Elvdal with a younger boy after a raid four days ago. The raiders killed everyone in Elvdal and then went toward the river. We are trying to reach Fjellheim. My friend is cold and hungry and maybe sick. I was hunting when I saw your son and the wolves."

The woman looked silently at Sigurd and then put her hand on his arm. "I spoke hastily, Sigurd, and I am sorry. You saved my son. Thank you." She looked into Sigurd's eyes. "I am Asah, and this is Ragnar. We are going home to Fjellheim. I came to Elvdal with my husband to get Ragnar. He had spent the winter there with my husband's parents. The day before the raid, Ragnar took me downstream to see the waterfall, which he loved, and we camped there. We saw the fires and the raiders as we returned in the morning. We hid until they went east. We wept as we walked through the village. Then we started home."

She paused and then said quietly, "My husband and his parents were in Elvdal when the raiders came. We searched but did not find them."

"My mother and father and brother and sister were there," Sigurd said. "I was out gathering wood. So was my friend." He looked at her pack. "Do you have food? I am afraid for him. He is cold and weak."

"I have food, and I will try to help your friend. Then you will both come with me to Fjellheim and stay with my family."

"Thank you for your kindness. If you don't have enough food for that journey, we could cook and eat the wolf."

"I would rather eat the straps of my pack. I have plenty of food."

Sigurd stooped over the body of the wolf and retrieved his arrow. Then he led Asah and the boy Ragnar toward the camp where Gunnar waited.

SIGURD HAD NOT KNOWN Gunnar well. Gunnar was four years younger, the same age as Sigurd's younger brother Kani. Gunnar and Kani had often played together when they were small—their mothers had been friends as children. But Kani sickened and died at age six, and after that Sigurd saw Gunnar only occasionally.

Gunnar was small for nine, and Sigurd's concern for him was well founded. Gunnar had lost his family and had seen too much horror and gone too long without warmth or food. Sigurd saw him curled quiet and pale on the ground and feared he might have died. Gunnar did respond, if barely, when Sigurd shook his shoulder, but then lapsed back into sleep, or near-sleep, and Sigurd could not rouse him.

Asah knelt by the boy, her face near his. Then she straightened up. "Sigurd, I think he's simply hungry and cold. Can you build a fire?"

The ground was clear of snow underneath the overhanging rock. Once the fire flared to life, Gunnar stirred toward it. Asah opened her pack, and Sigurd saw that it contained many dried plants. Asah took a small pot from her pack, filled it with water and crushed a leaf into it, and put it near the fire. While it heated, she crushed a different leaf, rubbing her hands together, and then stroked Gunnar's face and head. Gunnar's eyes opened, and he looked from Sigurd to Asah in apparent confusion. Asah reached beneath him, lifted him a little, and brought the pot of warm liquid to his mouth. "Drink this."

Gunnar drank, sighed, and lay back. "I thought I was dying, but now I'm hungry. We didn't eat at all yesterday."

"Your spirit is suffering from the loss of your family," Asah said, "and your body from cold and hunger, but you are a strong boy, and once you have had enough to eat you will feel better." She reached into her pack. "I have venison for a few days for all of us."

By noon the sun broke through the clouds, and the day began to warm. The woman and the three boys rested and ate, and the companionship they provided each other soothed their grief. "If the weather clears," Asah said, "we could be in Fjellheim tomorrow. With snow on the ground it would take two or three days, but I suspect tomorrow will be warm and dry."

3

SIGURD WALKED AHEAD of Asah and the two younger boys and reached the mountain pass by late morning, well before them. Alone in that high place under a cloudless sky of a color seen only in the far north, he looked over the longest view of his life—a descending canyon opening southeastward to his first sight of the distant sea. He knew it immediately for what it was; his father had described this place to him so clearly that he felt he had seen it himself.

He had climbed the steep snowy trail in cold morning shadow, but the gentler canyon ahead lay in full sun, its snow cover burned away. A group of deer browsed below, and occasional swatches of springtime color relieved the starkness of the alpine view. A stream trickled from a small tarn not far below him, nestled at the foot of a snowpack that extended upward into a side canyon. He descended to sit beside the tarn and waited for the others to catch up. The water was a blue even deeper than the sky it reflected, and where water met snowpack, the ice was a deep blue-green. Remembering his father's delight at this place brought Sigurd back to his present reality, and he silently prayed for the spirits of his family.

Asah found him so lost in thought that he didn't hear her approach. She had labored up the climb in grieving silence, but reaching the pass had lifted her spirits, for she was nearly home. When she saw Sigurd sitting forlornly beside the stream, her heart went out to him. Losing his family at thirteen seemed a catastrophe even worse than her own, for he was alone and homeless, while she was surrounded by boys who felt like family.

She sat beside Sigurd. "We won't reach Fjellheim until late afternoon, but the going will be easy, downhill and with a good path." As the four of them rested and ate, ground squirrels peered out of holes in the meadow below, and the day's first breeze stirred the new grass.

THE SUN WAS LOW when they reached Fjellheim. All afternoon the boys had followed Asah through evergreen forests that grew sparsely on both sides of the stream. The canyon was narrow and steep in places, but near Fjellheim the slope gave way to level land. Beyond the village lay its fields, not yet green that early spring. In the afternoon sunlight their freshly-turned ground stood out dark against the sky.

Sigurd was surprised to see that Fjellheim was even smaller than Elvdal, nothing more than a tiny cluster of houses along the stream. Asah's house stood near the upstream end of the village, and she was glad to see it even though coming home without her husband wrenched her anew. Inside, a stone hearth occupied the center of a large single room. In one corner of the front stood a table with bench seats. Asah's sleeping pallet was against the back wall, near Ragnar's. During Asah's absence, her older son, Oddi, had stayed with her sister in the adjoining house, and he remained there now, to make room for Sigurd and Gunnar, who set up their sleeping pallets in the front of the room.

From the ceiling hung many dried plants. Outside, at the top of the streambank, Asah kept a small vegetable garden, her pride, though not yet planted this year. "The year Ragni was born," she said, "the stream flooded, and the water was over the bank for days. Since then the garden has produced the best crops since I first planted it."

"You are kind to take us in," Sigurd said, in this home that was his own now, but not his own.

Asah looked steadily at him. "I am lucky to have met you."

AT THE CEREMONY of the midsummer moon in Fjellheim, Asah presented Sigurd and Gunnar to the village and told the stories surrounding their arrival—of the raid on Elvdal and the massacre of its inhabitants, of the loss of Asah's husband and Sigurd's and Gunnar's families, and of Sigurd saving Ragnar. None of this was new to the villagers, but in the ritual telling the events became part of the village's formal history, to be retold every year. Asah was the speaker not because she was personally involved, but because recounting that history was her duty as an elder.

As Sigurd and Gunnar stood before the assembly in the moonlight, she saw they had filled out, living with her and eating well. Gunnar was no longer the pathetic waif she had first met, and he had formed friendships with her son Oddi and her sister's son Orn, both Gunnar's age. Oddi and his cousin looked like blond twins.

Sigurd had turned fourteen and was noticeably taller than he had been fifty days before. Asah thought him a good fit for Fjellheim. He had joined the men hunting soon after he arrived, and on his first hunt he killed a buck. The men appreciated his skill with bow and arrow and the courage he showed by killing a wolf to save Ragnar. "He will grow to be a man of power," one said to Asah.

"He is that already. He saved Gunnar and Ragni. He is an unhappy boy, though, grieving for his family."

Sigurd's buck had yielded meat, bone, and hide— also sinew, which Sigurd would use for bowstring and to bind arrowheads. Gunnar had arrived in Fjellheim without bow and arrows. Soon after their arrival, he and

Sigurd had gone into the forest, returning with several straight beech branchlets for arrows and a fine strong dry branch of red oak for a bow, perfectly curved. Gunnar had shaped the bow and carved wooden points on three practice arrows. When the sinew was cured, Sigurd assembled the bow and the two boys made an archery range in the forest. Sigurd was disappointed by Gunnar's lack of skill, but Gunnar practiced daily and by midsummer was already stronger and more proficient. Sigurd showed him how to flake arrowheads and secure them to arrows, and Gunnar worked on arrowheads every morning. His confidence jumped when he shot a rabbit with his own bow and an arrow he had made himself. At the midsummer ceremony he came before the assembly carrying his bow and arrows with pride.

BY THE TIME OF THE CEREMONY of the midsummer moon, every one of Fjellheim's sixty inhabitants knew Sigurd and Gunnar well. One man at the ceremony, however, knew nothing of the two boys—Elder Hjari, visiting from the much larger village of Kystenlandsbyen, a center of boat building and metalwork on the seacoast to the east. He had walked a full day to Fjellheim to bring news of raids on the coast and discuss Kystenlandsbyen's plan to defend itself. He met with the elders of Fjellheim on the day of the ceremony to inquire about young men willing to help defend the coast.

"Sooner or later, the raiders will move south along the coast," Elder Hjari said. "They would not yet attack a village the size of Kystenlandsbyen, but they could overwhelm the small villages north and south of us, and we would be lost. For all of us, the only safety lies in a guard force made up of men from all the nearby villages. Fjellheim is only a day's walk from the coast. How long would it last if Kystenlandsbyen fell?"

At the ceremony, Sigurd caught Elder Hjari's attention as a strong young refugee from a raid and a promising recruit. The elder mentioned Sigurd to Asah, and she brought Sigurd to him before dawn the following morning.

"Elder Hjari," she said with a deferential bow of her head, "here is Sigurd, from Elvdal. You heard his tale in the ceremony last night. He has lived with me since the raid on Elvdal." Asah then retired from the room.

Elder Hjari clasped Sigurd's arms. "Sigurd, I sorrow to hear of the raid on Elvdal and of the deaths of your family members. The raids are barbaric, and we must stop them."

Sigurd stood almost as tall as the elder and looked him in the eye. "Sir, I am honored that you think me capable of helping." Sigurd had of course already heard why Elder Hjari had come to Fjellheim and that he wanted to speak to Sigurd. Villages of sixty have few secrets.

"The reports of your courage and skill go before you, Sigurd. I hear that you are already a fine bowman and hunter, and could become a leader of men. I offer you a chance to be trained as a warrior, and perhaps to avenge your family."

Sigurd paused for thought before speaking. "I owe much to Asah. She brought me here and has housed me and fed me for nearly two months. I appreciate your offer, but I must speak with her before I give you an answer."

"My work here is done. I will return to Kystenlandsbyen later this morning. I hope you will decide to come there yourself. When you do, come to me first, and I will make arrangements for your food and housing."

"Are you traveling alone, sir?"

"I am traveling with Vadi, who has agreed to fight for Kystenlandsbyen."

Sigurd knew and liked Vadi, one of the village's hunters.

"If I am to come, I would like to travel with you. I will speak to Asah and return with an answer before the sun is fully risen."

SIGURD WAS ASTONISHED to find tears in Asah's eyes. She looked at him with a wry smile. "Another loss, and each one a fresh wound. When Fridrek died I thought my life was over. Then you killed the wolf and saved Ragni, and

I realized what I had to live for. In another time, without war, you would have stayed and changed Fjellheim with new blood and new ideas. I feel I'm losing a son, and that is my sorrow."

They looked at each other at length and embraced. "You saved our lives too," Sigurd said. "I was in despair when we met, and Gunnar was dying. I was fortunate to come here and live in your house as your son. I will never forget that. In any case, I will return every winter, and I will visit whenever I can. If Elder Hjari could walk here from Kystenlandsbyen in a day, I could do it in a morning, to see you."

"You are an unusual fourteen-year-old, Sigurd, for your depth as well as your courage and skill. I fear that as a warrior you could become coldhearted. But I see that you are destined to follow this path, that losing your family is the beginning of some new life. May you find what you seek."

"And you, Asah. Goodbye, and thank you."

Sigurd found Gunnar as soon as he had gathered his few things. "I'm going, Gunnar. I would not have left you when you needed me, but now you are safe, and I have something I must do."

"Will I never see you again?"

"Of course you will. I'll be nearby often, and I'll come here to visit. And I'll live here in the winter. You and Asah are the only family I have."

Later that day, walking toward Kystenlandsbyen with Vadi and Elder Hjari, Sigurd thought about parting from Asah and remembered her sadness. He had not shed a tear since the raid on Elvdal and the loss of his family—even including his mother, the warmest and most treasured person in his life, and his sister, whose happy laugh he would never forget. He did not dare open the door to those sorrows, and he wondered whether that numbness would follow him into the new life Asah foresaw.

4

"LEAVE? SIGURD, I HOPE you're not serious." After a halfmonth in Kystenlandsbyen, Sigurd had sought out Vadi for advice.

"Vadi, you can see how much bigger the men are than I, and stronger, and faster. Wouldn't I slow the group down in a fight? Shouldn't I go back to Fjellheim for a year or two first?"

"That would be fine if the raiders would wait for you to grow up." At sixteen, Vadi stood half a head above Sigurd. "I would rather have one smart and brave fourteen-year-old who has good reason to fear and hate the raiders than two grown men who don't. And no one will have to wait for you. Think of the stick fight."

Sigurd's group had paired off two days earlier in a mock-combat exercise, using sticks the length of a man's forearm in place of knives. Garnall, the old warrior who had fought raiders thirty years before and now supervised the training, taught the men how to thrust and parry. He emphasized that swinging with a knife necessarily exposes one to being stabbed. That lesson came hard to men who had learned to fight while drinking and usually resorted to roundhouse swings, but Sigurd caught on right away. He bested each of his partners repeatedly with lightning reflexes and competitive determination.

Sigurd's delight was short-lived. The next day the group had raced through a forest, and Sigurd didn't stand a chance, because the older men had longer legs and better endurance. Sigurd was embarrassed and discouraged.

"Remember," Vadi said, "when we were hunting together, you killed the buck, not I. Hunting is a good way to learn about a man. What I learned about you is that I'd rather not fight you."

"I feel the men don't like me and don't want me around. I'm afraid it's because they think they'll have to watch over me."

"If a fourteen-year-old defeats you in a stick battle, do you resent him because you think he'll be a burden? Every one of them knows you'll be a good fighter. It's tough to lose to someone smaller and younger. Your marksmanship is hard enough on them. The stick battle humiliated them."

Four men entered the room—three fighters from Sigurd's group and Garnall, who stopped to talk to

Sigurd. "You must not take it too hard that they outrun you. They're running the fastest they ever will. You'll be faster in a year and faster yet in two."

Sigurd wondered whether Garnall had overheard the exchange with Vadi. "Why did you think I was taking it hard?"

Garnall laughed. "I saw your face. Go easier on yourself. You'll do fine."

KYSTENLANDSBYEN was the biggest settlement in the area, home to more than fifteen hundred—enormous compared to Fjellheim, with its nine houses, or Elvdal, with twelve. The harbor was home to six boatyards, including two large ones that produced cargo boats. The marketplace, a trading center for fish, livestock, produce, and metal goods, attracted farmers from the entire region, which included more than a dozen small villages. Four coastal hamlets lay within a day's walk to the north, and a three-day walk southward would reach six more. Other villages, including Fjellheim, were inland on coastal streams. The total population of the small villages was less than half that of Kystenlandsbyen.

The elders saw this entire region as their sphere of defense. They had been recruiting from the outlying villages for three years, since the first news of renewed raids came by boat from the north. That effort had brought them two dozen fighters, and from

Kystenlandsbyen itself came sixty-five more. The Elvdal raid, the closest by far, had redoubled the recruiting effort, which was now Elder Hjari's sole task.

Two days to the north, behind a high headland, was the mouth of the river that flowed east from Elvdal. No village was located there, because the river delta flooded regularly in spring. The headland commanded a fine view north and west, and a watch had been posted there since early spring. Soon after the Elvdal raid, watchmen had seen the raiders walking downriver to the coast. To the watchers' relief, the raider group turned north, away from Kystenlandsbyen.

Sigurd and Vadi learned all this from Garnall. "Next time maybe they'll turn south, and eventually they will surely come here. We will keep a watch on the headland. If the raiders appear, we can be there in time to keep them from descending from the hilltop. The path down is steep and tricky, easy to defend."

THE FIGHTERS who did not live in Kystenlandsbyen slept on pallets placed in a neat row in a community building that had been used for boats and fishing equipment and smelled strongly of the sea. Four of Sigurd's training group slept there, along with a dozen fighters who had already completed Garnall's training. The rest of the trainees lived locally and slept at home.

Food for the fighters came from communal stores, which were at a low ebb when Sigurd arrived in midsummer but grew quickly during the fruit and grain harvests. The men often ate fish, which was new to Sigurd, and initially he would not touch it. Eventually hunger overcame his distaste, and he soon looked forward to fish as a good alternative to mutton, which was standard fare. Sheep were raised all along the coast, and sheep farmers were eager to help feed the growing army.

The elders had ample trade goods to pay for the needs of the fighters, because Kystenlandsbyen was a center of metalwork. Gravel beds in the nearby hills yielded greenish rock from which redmetal was extracted by heating. Redmetal—a lustrous dark red material that could be cast and hammered into strong, lightweight blades and ornaments—had been the focus of the village for generations, and metal weapons and ornaments made in Kystenlandsbyen were widely prized. Trading boats plied the inland sea carrying redmetal goods, returning with materials that were needed locally—flint, grain, lime, and hemp, and occasionally glarestone, a glossy black stone that could be fashioned into the sharpest edges and points. This trade nurtured the local economy, which supplied food and fighting knives—short swords—for the men. The fighters still used flint-headed arrows, which they made themselves from flint supplied by the elders, and many felt that the extra heft of the stone arrowhead provided an advantage that lightweight redmetal points could not match.

Training for combat involves learning many skills, but fighters must first be strong and hardy, because fighting means running. Sigurd and his cohort trained by running while wearing heavy packs—Sigurd's lighter than the others but heavy nonetheless. The men ran every morning—in the rain, through underbrush, in the mud, along the beach in the sand, and up the canyon toward Fjellheim. Sigurd was always exhausted by the end of the run and at first was barely able to get through the afternoon, but boys of fourteen recover quickly, and he adjusted. He was growing as well, fast becoming his imposing adult self. He later joked that he might have been taller if he hadn't spent all those mornings carrying a pack half his weight. By summer's end he was two fingers taller than when he arrived at midsummer and immensely strong for fourteen.

The training also taught marksmanship with bow and arrow, wrestling, and hand-to-hand fighting with clubs, knives, spears, and shields. Sigurd was naturally athletic and excelled at these, particularly archery. Soon he was supervising the regular evening archery practice and teaching others to make arrows and arrowheads, skills he had learned from his father, a carver and stone knapper.

SIGURD WAS BY FAR the youngest fighter in Kystenlandsbyen. The men in his training group admired his energy and athleticism, but some of the other fighters resented him, and trouble erupted on a hot night two months into the training. The day had been long. The evening meal was mutton stew, cooked by a local woman employed by the elders. Sigurd had enjoyed mutton all his life. The cook liked him, and he always did well when food was served.

Walking from the cook's hearth to a bench seat, carrying his stew, Sigurd tripped over an extended foot and fell forward, breaking the pottery bowl. Looking up, he saw that it was Farald who had tripped him, a regular fighter, not in the training group. Farald was from Hvit Elv, a small village south of Kystenlandsbyen. He was a large man, and red faced. He might have been drinking.

Farald smirked. "You're so good, lick that up."

The cook arrived, angry. "You tripped him!"

"He fell. He's too stupid to walk straight. He lurched my way and fell over my foot. I never moved it."

After the cook left, Sigurd asked, "Why did you do that?" In fact he already knew the answer: two days earlier, Farald had failed badly in an archery exercise Sigurd led.

"One more word and you'll get much worse. You think being able to shoot makes you a warrior? You make us all sick. If you were a man, I'd break you, but no, I can't, you're a *boy*. Afraid to fight."

A crowd had gathered. Garnall came up behind Farald and put a hand on his shoulder. "That's enough."

Farald twisted angrily away and stormed out of the building. Sigurd cleaned up the mess, got more stew, and sat with Vadi.

"Did you see it happen?"

"Yes. I even saw him beforehand, getting in place to trip you."

"Others apparently dislike me too. This is why I thought of returning to Fjellheim."

"Sigurd, you're new to an established group. You're young, and the men envy your ability. You'll win them over."

"What do you think I should do about Farald?"

"You'll have to fight him, I suppose. That's what usually happens. He will ambush you some night and try to hurt you."

"He surprised me this time. I'll have to be more aware."

TWO DAYS LATER, Garnall was in an unusually good mood when he spoke to Sigurd's group after the midday meal. "You're all doing well. Evenly matched and the equal of the regular fighters."

The day was cool and rainy, and the morning run had been a messy affair. The group had arrived muddy and laughing and had rinsed in seawater before the meal.

"I want to hold a stick battle tournament," Garnall went on, "for everyone who is able-bodied. I want the entire group to see you're ready for battle. We'll do it tomorrow."

Garnall spoke about the tournament to Haefnir, the battle leader of the Seacoast Guard, as the elders called the fighters. Haefnir agreed, and the men ended that day in excited anticipation.

AFTER BREAKFAST, Garnall divided the men into twenty-four groups of three. Stick battle was a two-man contest. The winner had to knock his opponent down or thrust the stick into his midsection or throat, inflicting a painful defeat but no real injury. Within each group of three, two would fight while the third observed. The loser traded places with the observer, and the victor fought on. When a fighter won twice in succession he was declared the winner of that group of three.

All twenty-four contests took place at once. Fighters were scattered noisily around the expansive archery range. Sigurd's quick reflexes and agility made him a superb stick battler. Within his training group of nine, only Vadi was his equal. Sigurd easily won his first round, battling two men who were ten years older and not nearly as fast.

For the second round, Garnall divided the winners into eight groups of three. Again, all the contests took place at once. Sigurd was grouped with Vadi and Hunding, a young man from Kystenlandsbyen. The three were evenly matched. Sigurd lost to Hunding, but Vadi beat Hunding, and Sigurd beat Vadi. Sigurd then fought Hunding again; the battle went on at length, continuing after all the other second-round battles finished. Eventually Sigurd won with a lightning jab to the abdomen. He clasped arms good-naturedly with Vadi and Hunding and sat down gratefully to rest.

Garnall then randomly divided the eight second-round winners into four pairs. These pair fights would take place one at a time, before the entire group. Sigurd was disquieted to see that he would face Farald, who glared at him with obvious malice before their fight came up. Farald was a large and muscular man, and Sigurd knew he would have to rely on speed. He also knew that Farald would be his first left-handed opponent.

When Garnall called Sigurd and Farald into the fighter's circle, the group fell quiet; all knew of the mealtime confrontation. Farald looked at Sigurd balefully, mouthing an insult. At the signal to begin, Farald jabbed fiercely at Sigurd's chest. Sigurd parried with his stick and then had to duck to avoid a fast swipe at his head. Farald was quick, and the left-handed swing seemed to come from nowhere. As Sigurd ducked, he swung at Farald's leg, striking his knee and hurting him.

Farald backed away, enraged. "They should have given me a man to fight," he hissed. "You fight like an old woman." He lunged at Sigurd, who stepped aside, jabbing Farald under his arm and hurting him again. Farald's fury made him incautious. With all the strength of his enormous body, he aimed a club blow at Sigurd's head, a roundhouse swing, lightning fast. Sigurd was faster; he dropped to his knees and came up with his stick hard into Farald's belly. Farald fell, and the match was over.

Sigurd offered his hand to help Farald up, as was the custom. Farald grabbed Sigurd's hand and yanked him to the ground, forcing his head into the dirt. The crowd roared its disapproval, and men jumped in to separate the two. Sigurd emerged with a bloody face and sat down, hurt and dizzy. Farald screamed insults in mounting rage until he was led away.

The remainder of the tournament was anticlimactic. Sigurd quickly lost his fourth-round battle and sat with Vadi to mop his face during the championship fight. "You will undoubtedly hear more from Farald," Vadi said.

5

A RUNNER ARRIVED late in the morning of the following day, exhausted. He had left the headland guard post at first light. Watchmen had seen a substantial group approaching from the north, moving generally south along the coast but veering inland, apparently heading for the upriver ford. The group would reach the river by day's end and could cross the headland in one more day.

The midday meal had ended. The news interrupted preparations for the afternoon, and a general meeting followed.

"They won't cross the headland tomorrow," Garnall said. "They'll send scouts first and cross the next day. Or perhaps they'll go upriver instead and won't cross at all. Call Haefnir."

"I'm here." Haefnir had emerged silently from his private room. "We don't know how many we must face, so we will all go—today, so we can be in place before their scouts come to the hilltop. We will meet tonight at the guard quarters below the headland. You need not be there by sundown; we will have moonlight for walking. I will leave immediately. You will overtake me, for my pace will be slow." He nodded to the men and left to supervise the loading of the Seacoast Guard's bullock cart, its pride, a large and deep box on wooden wheels that turned on a single axle. A dozen men could not carry its load.

Garnall spoke to the training group. "I'm not going. I'm too old to keep up. Vadi will be in charge. You'll go together. You'll need to hurry, because you must arrive before the main group. When you reach the guard quarters, proceed to the top of the headland to serve as advance scouts. Camp on the hilltop, well out of sight. Perhaps you can surprise the raider scouts tomorrow morning. Go to the armory and get your equipment. You'll leave right away."

The men were tired from their daily run, but their collective groan was mixed with excited chatter. Sigurd was eager for his first battle mission and didn't mind the exertion. After two months, he was fit and strong, and his traveling pack would be lighter than his daily training load. At the armory, he received a fighting knife with a razor-sharp redmetal blade. He had his bow and two dozen of his own arrows but did not carry a club. Garnall had advised him to avoid close combat if possible and to use mostly bow and arrow to survive against taller men with longer arms. Sigurd slung a large shield over his pack and walked outside to join the group, and before the sun was beyond the zenith, eight men and a fourteen-year-old boy, all carrying big packs, trotted north between the houses of Kystenlandsbyen and then along the packed sand of the beach, looking from a distance like a row of children playing Follow the Leader.

A DAY'S WALK FOR A MAN is one story; the same walk for a man hurrying with a heavy pack is entirely another, especially after a hard morning run. When the training group passed Haefnir and the creaking, groaning bullock cart in midafternoon, he saw the men's exhaustion and told them to rest at the guard station until first light before setting out for the hilltop.

They arrived in early evening. The fighter in charge greeted them.

"You're the training group?"

"Yes," Vadi said. "We're to sleep now, until first light. We need it."

"We heard you would go straight to the hilltop." A runner had arrived earlier with Haefnir's instructions.

"Haefnir changed his mind when he saw we were spent. He was afraid we would die," he added with a laugh, "and he thinks the raider scouts can't possibly be there until midmorning."

The guards shared their evening meal of mutton and then showed the group to a room with a hide-covered floor, where the men could lay out sleeping pallets.

AFTER DINNER, Sigurd and Vadi went outside to talk before bed. The moon cast long shadows, and the sound of the surf surrounded them.

Vadi asked, "Are you nervous?"

Sigurd was thoughtful. "Not at all. It's strange, but I feel numb inside even after four months. Are you?"

"Yes, very. I guess I'm a hunter, not a warrior, after all."

"Not nervous, little boy?"

Farald's voice came from behind them. "Aren't you afraid of being hurt, without your mother here to help?"

Vadi and Sigurd turned. Farald stood twenty paces from them in the moonlight, idly swinging a lethal-looking battle club.

"Farald," Vadi said, "you know better than to cause trouble. We have a job to do."

"Ignore him," Sigurd said. "I doubt he actually wants to fight." Sigurd had been prepared for a fight with Farald since the stick battle.

Farald's answer was a headlong charge. Sigurd notched an arrow and drew his bow.

Farald stopped. "You would shoot me down? I knew you were a coward!"

"Do you still want to fight?" Sigurd was not taunting; the question was serious.

Farald turned and walked away, and Sigurd lowered his bow. A dozen paces away, Farald whipped around and flung a knife. Sigurd jumped aside, and the blade passed through the fleshy part of his upper left arm instead of his chest. He quickly pulled the knife out and tossed it aside. His arm was bleeding and painful. He could no longer draw his bow and would have to face Farald with his fighting knife. As he drew it from his belt, Farald charged with his own fighting knife, using it like a club, swinging viciously. Sigurd danced aside, but the blade swept across his right forearm and left a long cut. Blood now ran down both of Sigurd's arms.

Farald turned and aimed a lunging swing at Sigurd's throat. Sigurd ducked underneath and brought his knife up into Farald's midsection. Farald collapsed onto his back with a grunt.

A long moment passed. Farald did not stir.

Sigurd retrieved his knife. "Vadi, can you help me bind my cuts?" Vadi took Sigurd's arm and led him into the guard station.

"What happened?" the guard asked.

"I stabbed a man who attacked me. Farald."

HAEFNIR HEARD THE STORY of the fight when he arrived later in the evening. He summoned Sigurd and looked at him gravely. "Why?"

"He attacked me four days ago at the evening meal and again at yesterday's stick battle. Tonight he searched me out and ran at me, but when I drew my bow he stopped and walked away. Then he turned and threw a knife, drew his fighting knife, and charged. I defended myself with my own fighting knife. I was lucky to escape with these." He held out his bandaged arms. "He hated me because earlier this month he did poorly in an archery practice I supervised and because I defeated him in the stick battle."

Haefnir closed his eyes to think. "I heard about the mealtime incident," he said at last, "and the stick battle. Garnall suspected that Farald might attack you when he had the chance. I think you acted reasonably. You will go with your group to the hilltop, wounded or not. And if you are involved in another such incident I will conclude that you provoke men to fighting."

Vadi's questions were more personal. "What did you think when he came at you with the knife? Weren't you afraid?"

"No. I told you—I haven't felt anything since the raid on Elvdal. I simply thought, 'Stab. Don't swing.' If Farald had remembered that, he could have killed me. I could never have escaped his long arms. I'm glad he's gone, but I feel no triumph."

"I saw you there, bleeding, your arm hanging down, and gave you up for dead. The fight ended before I had time to react. Every man at this guard station thinks you're a hero, beating a man twice as heavy and much taller."

"My first battle. I thought I was here to fight raiders."

THE GUARDS CAME THROUGH the sleeping area before first light and roused the fighters. Sigurd's right arm was healing, but the left was throbbing and swollen.

The guard who woke him raised an eyebrow. "You should dip that in seawater several times a day to keep it from festering."

Sigurd soaked his arm in the sea while the others ate breakfast. He bound it again with Vadi's help, quickly downed a bowl of gruel, and rushed out to catch up with his group. His pack was lighter than before, with only his weapons and a little food. His left arm was painful, but otherwise he felt as strong as ever—and relieved that the threat of ambush by Farald was no more.

The sun rose as the fighters reached the hilltop. One of the guards stationed there motioned them to the rock outcrop from which he was spying on the raiders. "Only about twenty of them. They camped across the river, singing and shouting until late last night. Now they're quiet."

The raider camp was far away, and Sigurd strained to see details. "They're dousing their fires and packing up to leave. Should we send a runner down?"

"No," Vadi said, "let's see what they do first. They haven't sent scouts here."

The raiders gathered in a group, obviously talking about which way to go. Sigurd could see the rocky river crossing downstream from them. They continued their discussion for some time and then shouldered their packs and walked upriver.

"They're going west!" Sigurd exclaimed.

The guard laughed. "Good news. And unexpected."

6

SIGURD'S FIRST SEASON with the Seacoast Guard passed without a battle with the Raiders from the North. The raider group that had headed west up the river returned a month later herding stolen livestock, and Sigurd's group again hurried to the headland to watch the outlaws turn north and walk up the coast. Only forty fighters made that trip, because Haefnir knew how many raiders they might face.

Snow fell in earnest a halfmonth later, and the fighting group in Kystenlandsbyen disbanded until spring. Vadi and Sigurd walked to Fjellheim the next day. Asah and Gunnar met them halfway. "I knew you would come today," Asah said happily, and then, "Sigurd! You are so much *bigger*."

"Maybe so," Vadi said, "but I've been losing weight. The food in Kystenlandsbyen includes too much fish. I'm looking forward to pork and mutton."

"You can have them tomorrow night at the celebration of your return."

Gunnar turned to Sigurd. "You killed a man." He was wide eyed.

"How did you learn about that?"

"Do you remember Einar? The hunter? His brother lives in Kystenlandsbyen. He came here last month and told us the story."

"It's nothing to boast of. I had to fight, or he would have killed me."

"Your friends are boasting quite a lot." Gunnar's eyes were full of hero worship.

Gunnar too had grown. He was eager to show Sigurd his skill with bow and arrow and proposed a shooting contest, saying, "If I win, can I hunt with you?" The contest had predictable results, but Sigurd praised him for his improvement and promised to take him hunting before winter ended.

Vadi and Sigurd continued to run with packs all winter, when the snow cover permitted. "Running was painful at first," Vadi said. "I never again want to start over." The two of them undertook long hunting trips by themselves, with remarkable success, beginning on the first trip, when they killed a bear. They butchered it on the spot. Vadi stayed to guard the meat; Sigurd carried a load to Fjellheim and returned with two more hunters to bring the rest back. Asah was overjoyed about the bear. The carcass was laden with fat, enough to see

Fjellheim through the winter, when lean rabbit and deer meat alone will not keep people healthy.

As spring approached, Sigurd kept his promise to take Gunnar hunting. They had not hunted together since the time of the Elvdal raid a year before. The weather was unexpectedly cold, and they were chilled by a late snowfall. "Like the spring blizzard a year ago," Gunnar said, "when I thought I was dying." He remained an enthusiastic hunting partner and was elated to shoot a doe that Sigurd hazed toward him. When they returned to the village, laden with meat, he brought it to Asah in jubilant triumph.

That evening Asah spoke to Sigurd. "I know you're a fine hunter and fighter. You have a warrior's heart. I see you living in peace with a family of your own someday, but I wish you could live more gently at fourteen, and I hope Gunnar never follows you to Kystenlandsbyen."

IN SPRING, Garnall made Sigurd the archery instructor for the entire group. The Seacoast Guard had six new fighters that year. Sigurd and Vadi ran with them mornings, and Sigurd spent evenings with them in archery practice. The men saw Sigurd differently that year, because of the fight with Farald and because he was no longer a boy. Now a bearded fifteen-year-old, he was as tall as most of the men—not as heavy, but with the strength and agility of a wrestling champion. If some men still resented him, they kept it to themselves.

Over the winter in Fjellheim, Sigurd had made himself a new weapon, a lightweight war club with four stone points like arrowheads embedded in the tip. He brought it to Garnall. "Do you think I can swing a club now? Last year you said I was too small."

Garnall hefted the club and stood back to look at Sigurd. "I think it's good," he said finally. "Light enough for you to swing quickly, but the stone points add heft and look deadly. Have you practiced using it?"

Sigurd smiled. "All winter."

"You're a different fighter this year. Still lethal with the bow at long range, and I would hate to go in against that club. But try to stay far enough away that you don't need it. You're still not big enough for close-in fighting, if you have a choice."

A MONTH AFTER MIDSUMMER, breakfast was underway when a runner arrived from the headland and collapsed onto a bench. He had run in the moonlight since about midnight. "Raiders," he gasped. "Camped at the river crossing. Must have arrived at night. We didn't know until they built fires. Twenty fires. Could be sixty or seventy men."

Haefnir's sixth sense had brought him out of his private room to hear the runner's report. "They could have scouts at the headland by midday and could cross tomorrow morning. Twenty fires? We'll take everyone."

Garnall was like a mother hen getting the six new fighters ready to leave. They were to continue to the hilltop, as Sigurd's group had the year before.

Sigurd turned to Haefnir. "I would like to join them. Last year I had an idea up there, and I'd like to try it."

"Come to my room and tell me about it."

SIGURD ARRIVED AT THE GUARD QUARTERS in late afternoon with Vadi and the six new fighters. The guards remembered him from the fight with Farald. "The others are not far behind," Sigurd said. "Send them to the hilltop right away, and tell them to go silently." The eight then climbed to the headland without even stopping for a meal.

The headland rose steeply to a large windy flat area, bare of trees. All around it, the slopes were thickly forested. They led up to higher hills on the west, and down in three directions—toward the river on the north, the sea on the east, and the guard station, out of sight at the headland's southern base. That southward slope was precipitous, with cliffs concealed by tree cover.

As soon as the group reached the hilltop, one of the guards on watch came to Sigurd. "Six raider scouts came here at midday. We watched from up there." He pointed westward to a high rocky formation. "They stood right here, looking at the villages to the south. After they left, we returned to that outcrop." He gestured toward a second guard, who was looking northward from a jumble of rocks at the northeast edge of the hilltop, which commanded a view of the river. "The scouts rejoined the main group, which is about sixty strong. They had a long discussion. Now they're eating."

Sigurd followed the guard to the outcrop and looked across the river to a large encampment. A festive meal was underway, with many fires. Sigurd could faintly hear raucous singing.

When the main group of Haefnir's fighters arrived at the hilltop, Sigurd positioned them in hiding in the trees on both sides of the narrow south end. "Don't attack until I signal," he said.

Sigurd, Vadi, and the six new fighters camped in the open on the hilltop. They had brought four rabbit carcasses, which they hung in full view from a nearby branch to suggest they were hunters. Sigurd insisted they sleep fully dressed and ready to fight. "We won't have time to lace our boots in the morning. They will charge when they see us. We will run for our lives, with frightened shouting, to draw them to the south end."

Lying on his sleeping pallet that night, Sigurd stared at the twilit sky—even a month after midsummer, the sky was never fully dark—and wondered why he was so calm on the eve of his first major battle. He could be hurt or killed. No trace of fear, he thought. Would he ever know normal human feelings again?

WE ARE MORE than half a hundred heroes. None can resist us. We have slain all who stood in our path, and we shall sweep like windblown fire through the villages to the south.

We rise early and crest the hill before sunrise. A hundred paces ahead, a sleepy hunters' camp surprises us. Only yesterday afternoon, this hilltop was deserted. We break into a run. The hunters will not hear us, for hide footwear on hard turf is soundless. We hope to run down the campsite and its occupants, but one man sits up and sees us. We are only seventy paces from him and moving fast. He shouts an alarm that rouses the other men, but by the time all eight are on their feet, we are only forty paces away. They run, abandoning their equipment and leaving fresh-killed rabbit hanging from a tree. We can use all of that but will deal with the men first.

The hunters run directly south toward the steepest of the slopes descending from the hilltop. They hope to disappear into the forest and escape with their lives, but they are still far from the trees, and we are already within attacking range. An arrow brings down one of them, and another reaches for his hand to pull him out of harm's way. Too late! The leading heroes are upon them!

Without warning, the morning erupts in death, death from the trees to the east and west, a storm of arrows shot by dozens of hidden men. Some heroes turn back, but more men hidden in the forest bar a safe retreat. Hundreds of enemies! The hunters were bait!

Our leaders turn the group and run back to the north. They think at least to kill the man who is down; three converge on him with knives. But no! A battle-crazed boy is with him, wielding a club. He is possessed by spirits, and no ordinary man could match his strength. A dozen heroes aim arrows, but he moves so fast and with such rage that not one comes close. He charges the leaders, laying about himself with the club, killing right and left, a madman, a demon-possessed madman. He strikes dead our second leader. He stands by the downed man and drives off all the nearby heroes.

All the while deadly arrows fly from the trees, and more heroes fall mortally wounded.

Finally one of our arrows finds its mark, and the crazed madman is down, struck in the shoulder, but it is too late for us. Enemies charge from the trees, bent on killing. Only the lucky among us escape to plan our revenge. Almost three dozen heroes lie dead or dying.

ALWAYS AFTERWARD, Sigurd thought of that morning as the time he discovered battle frenzy. As a child, he had heard men talk about warriors so full of the fire of battle that they went beyond their normal abilities. For Sigurd, from the moment the raiders appeared, time slowed to a crawl. He never forgot an instant of the action.

Vadi fell, and Sigurd knew immediately that he must save his friend from death. He charged, feeling neither fear nor despair, and tried to pull Vadi into the trees, but the leading raiders came for him with stone-bladed knives. Sigurd felt invincible and immensely powerful, and fire was in his eyes. He lashed out with his club, and raiders fell. Then he felt a heavy blow to his shoulder and was confused to find himself on the ground. All around him men were running—his own men. They helped him to his feet and pulled the arrow from his shoulder. Vadi had taken an arrow in the lower leg. He had hit his head when he fell but was coming around. When he saw Sigurd's shoulder streaming blood, he passed out again.

Sigurd saw dozens of bodies—all raiders, none of the Seacoast Guard. Later he learned that three fighters died. The men had waited for his signal to charge, but when they saw him surrounded, they took the initiative upon themselves.

Afterward, Sigurd could recall the details of the clothing of the raiders he struck down but little of what happened after the battle. He remembered a healer from the nearest village treating him and Vadi in the guardhouse but could not have said how long he remained there. In fact it was almost a month before he and Vadi were fit to walk back to Kystenlandsbyen to receive the cheers and gratitude of the men Sigurd had led.

7

SIGURD AND VADI stayed in Kystenlandsbyen only long enough to gather their strength for the walk to Fjellheim—and for Vadi to convince Otama, a girl from Kystenlandsbyen, to come with them. Sigurd had originally thought Otama was simply another of the young women who flocked around the fighting men, but Vadi was quick to correct him. "She is nothing like that. I met her in the market when I went for greens for the cook. Otama has no family of her own. She helps at a sheep farm in exchange for room and board." Vadi promised her that his mother would take her in and already knew all about her. Of course that wasn't true, but Vadi loved her and was almost sure his mother would accept her. In any event, Otama was a sunny and beautiful companion as they walked slowly toward Fjellheim, Vadi still limping.

Asah was happy to see them although shocked by their wounds. She was warm and welcoming to Otama, as was Vadi's mother. Sigurd had brought Asah a goat cheese, one of many food gifts he had received for his part in the battle. By the time he and Vadi reached Kystenlandsbyen, the story of Sigurd's heroism was known by all, and Haefnir told the fighters it was Sigurd's plan that had turned the day. Even Garnall, tough old warrior that he was, was effusive in his praise.

THE WINTER IN FJELLHEIM was early and hard. Snow covered the ground long before the festival of spirits, at the full moon midway from equinox to midwinter, and after that snow fell daily for a halfmonth. The freak warm spell that followed compacted the snow cover, and then bitter cold left a hard icy surface. Deer tried pathetically to break the crust to browse, and Sigurd and Vadi enjoyed superb winter hunting.

Vadi spoke about his love for Otama and told Sigurd they would ask Asah to marry them at midwinter. "I'm learning about part of myself I didn't know. With her, I'm completely different from the hunter or the warrior on the hilltop." They sat by their fire at the end of another successful hunting day.

"I've been thinking more about that battle," he added. "I could have died, but what I remember is the excitement of it."

Sigurd too had been thinking about the battle. He remembered feeling fully alive in a way he had almost forgotten. Nearly two years had passed since the raid on

Elvdal, and for all that time he had felt dead—except for those few moments on the hilltop, when his every sense was acute and he was full of the fire of living. "It is good to be here, hunting," he said, "but I crave the energy I found on the hilltop."

Vadi looked at him at length. "Garnall says some men are meant to be warriors and are not fully themselves except when they're fighting."

"I hope that's not true of me. I don't want a life of killing. But I may have no choice. Asah says my path is dictated by destiny."

SNOW FELL AT THE CEREMONY of the midwinter moon. The wedding of Vadi and Otama was a happy event, and the gathering provided a welcome relief from the isolation of winter, when Fjellheim was cut off from the world by deep snow and its people were confined, staying warm by staying inside. Food stores were ample, for deer were plentiful, and all the hunters did well. Asah had harvested a large field of grain during the summer, with Gunnar's help, and the midwinter feast was rich. Vadi got drunk and regaled the assemblage with the story of the battle, singing Sigurd's praises in a song he had made up for the occasion. Asah retold the story of Sigurd saving Ragnar, now a growing eight-year-old who thought of Sigurd as a god-like hero.

Otama turned to Sigurd. "Last year in Kystenlandsbyen we talked about you because of your fight with Farald. This year you led us to victory over many raiders. And you're so young!"

SPRING WAS LATE AND STORMY, and Sigurd did not leave for Kystenlandsbyen until nearly midsummer. Asah spoke from her heart as he left. "I fear a difficult summer for you, Sigurd." Her hands were on his shoulders. "I see that you want battle and are not afraid of death, but I have a premonition of trouble. I will be relieved to see you again."

"Asah, I do not have your deep sight, but I am confident. And I will be cautious."

Sigurd was surprised and pleased that Vadi had decided to return to Kystenlandsbyen. "I have a wife, and she is with child. But fighting will make it less likely that she will die at the hands of raiders, and my dreams tell me I will return safely."

At Kystenlandsbyen, Sigurd and Vadi were saddened to learn that Garnall had died over the winter, aged almost fifty-five. Haefnir selected another older fighter as chief of training. Elder Hjari too had died, aged sixty, leaving Haefnir with a problem of another sort. As a result, he spoke to Sigurd.

"After such a defeat, I think the raiders will not appear this season. One of Elder Hjari's tasks was maintaining contact with the villages to the south, and we must continue that. I want you to choose a few men—two should be enough—and lead them south.

Visit every village. Ask the elders whether they have young men who could join us. Many of those villages are on coastal streams; ask whether other villages lie upstream, and visit them too. Walk up each stream in any event, to look at possible raider routes to the coast. I doubt the raiders will try to cross the headland again anytime soon."

"I will do my best." In truth, Sigurd was disappointed. The battle on the hilltop repeated itself in his dreams night after night along with the intensity he had felt there, and he had hoped for more fighting, although he too realized the raiders would probably not return this season.

"Your voice betrays your feelings, Sigurd, but you will need to know all the work I do. You should realize that you will lead the Seacoast Guard at some point."

"Sir? I am sixteen years old. Your job requires a more experienced man."

Haefnir laughed. "I'm not planning to quit this year. But I want you ready to take over when I do. Recruiting fighters from the villages to the south will help you. Choose your men and begin." The two clasped arms and parted.

Sigurd sought out Vadi. "Haefnir wants me to take two men southward and visit those villages, as Elder Hjari did. Will you come with me?"

Vadi smiled broadly. He had already guessed what Haefnir and Sigurd were discussing. "I hoped you would ask. We should take Erland. He's from Hvit Elv, which we'll visit, and he knows that area well. He's older but smart and friendly. I got to know him after the fight with Farald. He had disliked Farald from childhood and says his death improved the world."

SIX VILLAGES LAY ON THE COAST south of Kystenlandsbyen; Hvit Elv was the farthest. Sigurd enjoyed traveling with Vadi and Erland, but his head was full of battle, and he found recruiting for the Seacoast Guard tiresome work. In the first month, the three emissaries visited seven villages—five on the coast, two upstream—with a population of about two hundred all told. Village men listened to Sigurd. He had filled out over the winter and was an imposing sight in battle gear—shield, bow, fighting knife, and his club with stone points. In some villages he was already known as the hero of last year's battle. He persuaded six young men to join the fighting force and sent them to Haefnir.

"You'll be known in Hvit Elv too," Erland said. "Not many liked Farald."

They were still a day's walk from Hvit Elv when Erland told them of a mountain village a half-day's walk up its stream—Fosser, which means waterfalls. "It would make sense to visit Fosser first. We could leave the coast now and climb to the high ridge and then come to Fosser from above. That way, we would avoid the nasty steep climb from Hvit Elv to Fosser."

They spent much of that morning climbing, following a canyon that was a continuous flower garden. Eventually they reached the ridge, where they followed a well-worn path toward Fosser. They enjoyed stunning views; from one point they could see all six coastal villages and, in the distance, Kystenlandsbyen. Fosser itself was in a canyon, and they could not see it until late afternoon, when they topped a ridge above it. The village lay at the confluence of three streams. "The waterfalls below Fosser are beautiful," Erland said. "I'll show them to you tomorrow."

They camped on the ridge, upstream from the village. Wolves howled in the night from the canyon near Fosser, and owls hooted nearby.

"SIGURD, WAKE UP." Vadi sounded alarmed.

The sun had not yet risen. Sigurd stood, groggy with sleep, and saw smoke rising from Fosser.

"Could it be raiders?" Erland stood beside them.

"Haefnir thought we would see no raiders this year," Sigurd said, "but smoke in early morning is a bad sign."

They packed quickly and ate on the move. By the time they had a clear view of Fosser, the village was fully in flames, and gangs of men ran from house to house, burning and killing. For Sigurd the scene was a chilling replay of Elvdal. He found himself standing in the forest with Gunnar again, unable to prevent the horror before his eyes. The impression was so strong that he had to struggle to pull himself back to the present.

"They must have come south on the other side of the mountains," he said. "Vadi, you're fastest. Run back the way we came and report to Haefnir as soon as you can. There's no hope for Fosser, and perhaps not for Hvit Elv, but if you hurry, Haefnir could reach the other villages in time to save them."

"What will you do?" Vadi was reluctant to leave.

"We'll go to Fosser to see if there's any way to help. Go. Go now. Lose no time."

Vadi left at a trot.

THE DESTRUCTION OF FOSSER was all but complete. The fire had spread to a hillside of dry timber south of the stream, and huge tongues of flame engulfed the ridge across the canyon from Sigurd and Erland. "Unlikely we can save anyone," Sigurd said. "Let's stay on the ridge until we're directly above the village."

They saw raiders gathering in a field below the village, herding stolen livestock. When the smoke shifted and blocked the view, Sigurd and Erland scrambled down to the canyon bottom and then walked upstream toward Fosser.

Sigurd froze, startled by a scream, and another, close by. Hurrying that way, he saw three men—the closest leading a goat, the others binding two young girls, whose terrified shrieking made so much noise that the raiders did not notice Sigurd. Motioning to Erland to follow, he silently charged. He brought his club down onto the head of the closest raider, and the man fell without a sound. A fourth raider appeared, and Erland charged him with fighting knife in hand while Sigurd turned toward the two girls and their captors.

Once again, as at the hilltop, time slowed for Sigurd. Fully alive, he saw everything in crystalline detail. He saw the fourth raider cut down Erland with a knife. Sigurd leapt at the raider and clubbed him to the ground, but Erland was beyond help. Then Sigurd felt a searing pain and looked down to see that an arrow had pierced his thigh. He stayed on his feet but was almost unable to move for the pain. As the two men advanced on him, Sigurd found strength beyond himself. He staggered toward the raiders and felled one with his club. The second hoisted one of the girls and fled with her as she screamed in terror.

Putting weight on his leg gave Sigurd pain so great that he felt faint. Struggling against passing out, he hobbled to the remaining girl, the younger of the two. She seemed unhurt and had stopped screaming. Sigurd quickly cut her ropes with his fighting knife.

"Can you walk?"

Her eyes were unseeing, wide with horror. Sigurd realized she was in shock.

"Come with me. They will return. We must hide."

Sigurd glanced around at Erland and the three raiders, all motionless. Then, with a hand pressed to his thigh in an attempt to hold back the blood and the pain, he took the girl's hand and hobbled upstream.

MY EARLIEST MEMORY is of Amma delivering a baby. I was three. That was the first time I had seen a birth, and the blood frightened me, but Gerde reassured me and told me bleeding was normal. The mother recovered, and the baby was fine, a beautiful little girl I will never forget.

I lived with my midwife grandmother Amma, my grandfather Afi, and my sister Gerde, who was three years older and knew everything. She and I kept the house clean, because Amma was often away for birthing and Afi was partly crippled. Amma was the only midwife in Fosser and sometimes even went to Hvit Elv to deliver babies. That was a half-day walk with a steep climb coming back, so Amma didn't go there in winter.

Amma was a healer and knew many spirit songs, which she taught to Gerde and me. She sang at festivals and ceremonies of marriage, and she sang the prayers when people died. Gerde and I had regular chores—

besides keeping house, we collected firewood, hauled water, and helped Amma at birthings. We had time to ourselves too. We fished in the stream canyons and admired the views. We loved the waterfalls downstream from the village and went there often, sometimes even by ourselves. Amma and Afi thought that was safe because the waterfalls were nearby and deserted. It's beautiful there in summer, and flocks of little birds come in the evening to catch insects.

We had gone to the waterfalls first thing in the morning. It was broad daylight, because it was summer and never dark. We were on our way back when we saw the fires. I started to run, but Gerde stopped me.

"We have to hide."

The look on her face told me something was terribly wrong. Then I heard screaming.

We ran into a stream canyon we knew well. We were behind a big tree when two men saw us. One grabbed me and tied me, and the other caught Gerde. They were rough looking and dark haired, and their words sounded like grunting.

I was shaking. I looked at Gerde and saw she was terrified. "I'm afraid for Amma and Afi," she said. "I'm going to pray."

9

SIGURD WAS LUCKY ENOUGH to find a hiding place quickly, still on the stream but behind a tangle of bushes. He wanted to be much farther away, but he heard men returning and knew he was out of time. He waded through dense brush, and the girl followed him to a sandy shore underneath an overhanging rock wall. They were completely concealed, and they remained still, barely breathing. Sigurd was in great pain.

Men searched back and forth along the stream, frighteningly close. It was midmorning before they gave up and went away. The girl started to speak then, but Sigurd held his finger to his lips and pointed outward through the bushes. Eventually, two more men stood, laughed, and walked away downstream. A single word would have given the hiding place away.

The arrow had passed completely through Sigurd's leg, above the knee. The girl watched with wide eyes as he broke off the protruding tail and pulled the arrow from his leg. He almost fainted from the pain. He reached into his pack for a scrap of hide, soaked it in the pool, and bound it to his leg to stop the bleeding.

He looked at the girl. "Are you hurt?"

She shook her head, sobbing. "What will happen to my sister?"

She looked into Sigurd's eyes, and his heart stopped, because she reminded him of his own sister, who also had long straight golden hair and blue eyes that showed no shyness.

Eventually she calmed. "What's your name?"

"Sigurd. What's yours? How old are you?"

"Inge. I'm almost ten. My sister is Gerde."

He smiled through his pain. "Well, Inge, I'm glad I found you. I'm sorry I couldn't save you both."

"Where did you come from? You're not from Fosser."

"I came from the north with two friends. We were coming to Fosser to speak to the elders. One of my friends is dead now. The other is going for help."

Inge said nothing, but new tears showed that she was thinking of what had happened to her grandparents and her sister.

THE RAIDERS RETURNED later that day, searching still, and the next morning. When they appeared no more, Sigurd guessed they had gone on to Hvit Elv. He was concerned about his wounds, which were red and swollen, and about food. "Inge, eat this." He handed her two pieces of dried venison from his food bag.

"What about you? What will you eat?"

"I'll hunt tomorrow morning. A grown man can go without food longer than a reed-thin nine-year-old girl."

She looked at Sigurd gratefully. "Thank you." She had not eaten for two days and was dizzy with hunger.

Sigurd was mopping his wounds with stream water when Inge looked at them. "Those could fester. You should put thyme on them."

"What will thyme do? How do you know about it?"

"My Amma was a healer." She sat down and started to cry. Sigurd sat beside her and put his arm around her shoulders, and she leaned gratefully against him for comfort, sobbing still.

When she recovered, she stood. "Wild thyme grows all around here." She led him to a shrub growing against the rock. Sigurd feared discovery, and they quickly retreated to their hiding place. He was in more and more pain.

"You're hurting," she said. "We have to find food, but you can't even walk for the pain. These willow leaves could help that." She reached out and plucked one. "Let me tend your leg."

Sigurd lay back and winced while she swabbed the wounds on both sides of his leg and rubbed thyme on them. Then she picked a fistful of willow leaves, plastered the wounds, and rebound the leg.

"You're very young to know about healing."

"My Amma taught me everything I know. She knew much more. I'm only learning."

"The pain is already better. Thank you."

SIGURD WOKE EARLY on the second day after the fight. He was weak with hunger and knew Inge must be as well, although she never complained. He gave her the last piece of venison, lurched unsteadily to his feet, and picked up his bow and arrows.

Inge stood beside him. "I'm hungry, but I'm afraid to be alone. What if they come back? You're not strong or steady. Couldn't I come with you? I could help you."

"You're safer here. If you don't move, they could never find you even if they did return. I wouldn't go, but we have to have food."

Inge sat, her jaw set.

"You're a brave girl. I'll be back soon." Sigurd hobbled out through the bushes, waded the stream, and painfully climbed the opposite bank. On the upper rim he sank down and leaned back against a tree, dizzy and exhausted. He may have fainted; he opened his eyes to find two rabbits browsing not twenty paces to his left—a gift, but not yet in hand, and he knew that even the slightest disturbance would spook his prey. Sigurd's bow was in his left hand, and the arrows were in the quiver on his back. Moving too slowly for any watcher to notice, he reached for an arrow, notched it, and drew the bow.

The rabbits remained unaware.

He was relieved to succeed. Pursuit was beyond his strength.

He found that Inge had not moved at all. "A rabbit!" She was grateful and delighted, and when she saw he could not kneel, she dressed the rabbit herself. She was about to build a fire when they froze at the sound of footsteps. Three men walked along the far bank of the stream, looking everywhere, occasionally stopping to listen. They passed close to where Sigurd had shot the rabbit and then walked away upstream. Some time later they passed by headed downstream.

SIGURD AND INGE spent the day in tense silence. By late afternoon they could go no longer without food. Inge laid a small fire and roasted the entire rabbit, piece by piece, on green sticks.

Food had never tasted so good.

After they ate, Inge inspected Sigurd's wounds. "Lie back, and I'll change the binding."

That night Sigurd dreamed of a little girl flying around his head as if it were perfectly natural. He looked closely, unsure whether she was his sister, or Inge, or perhaps both. She sang a song he had heard from his mother. He woke at first light in tears, his first in more than two years. Inge knelt over him, her eyes full of concern.

"Don't worry, Inge, it was only a dream. About my mother and my sister. I miss them."

"Dreams are important," she said gravely. "You can learn from them."

SIGURD FELT STRONGER in the morning, and his swelling and pain were down. He and Inge finished the last few pieces of rabbit, and Sigurd stood.

"We need to leave. This is the last place they saw us, and they will be back."

"Where will we go?"

"Up that way." He pointed toward the ridge he and Vadi and Erland had followed on their way to Fosser—in another life, a hundred years before. Now Erland was dead, Vadi gone, Sigurd disabled. He also had a dependent, a little girl with a healer's touch. She wasn't his sister, but her presence comforted the wound he had hidden from himself for two years, and he knew he must get her away from that place of death as fast as he could.

"I know that path," she said. "Gerde and I went there."

THE GOING WAS SLOW AND PAINFUL. Sigurd's left leg could not bear his weight; he found a stout stick to use as a cane. With Inge walking ahead, the two climbed out of the canyon on the same steep path Sigurd and Erland had used to walk into it. On the ridge, Sigurd recognized the campsite from which he had seen Fosser burning, and he saw the tracks Vadi had made on his way back out, scuffing every step as he ran.

By afternoon they reached the high ridge, with its commanding views. Sigurd was surprised and pleased to see Hvit Elv; he had feared that it would be a blackened ruin. He remembered deep gullies below the path and began looking carefully downhill for a place where he and Inge could camp safely. They needed it quickly; he was close to exhaustion.

"Look, Inge." He pointed to the bottom of a small stream canyon. "I will have to struggle to climb down there, but if we camp beyond that first bend, we couldn't be seen from up here. We'll keep our fires small. We'll have water from the stream, and I can hunt. We would be safe there until I'm strong enough to walk."

She looked at him with her wise eyes. "I've been there. There's a deep pool around that bend. I saw a deer there once. And we don't need to go down that steep slope. I know an easy path."

DEER DID COME TO THE POOL, and Sigurd killed a small buck early the following morning. He dressed the carcass a little at a time, resting when he tired. Inge built a fire and cooked their first real meal since the fight—all the venison they could eat, with berries Inge picked from a bush beside the stream.

"We'll be all right now," Sigurd said. "They won't find us here. We have food and water, and I have my own healer. We'll stay here until I'm strong enough to travel. Then we'll go to Fjellheim."

"Where's Fjellheim?"

"In the mountains above Kystenlandsbyen, six or eight days' walk from here. I know a woman there, a healer, who will help us."

"Oh, I know Kystenlandsbyen. My uncle went there to work on a fishing boat, but he sickened and died."

Later that day Sigurd came upon Inge sitting beside the pool, chin in hand, staring at nothing. He limped to her and sat down.

"My sister's name was Gudrun. She would have been nine now, too."

"Does it hurt to think of her?"

"I've tried not to, but I see her every time I look at you. You're helping me face that grief. I'm sorry for what happened to our families, but it was a kind fate that threw us together."

"You feel more like a father than an older brother. I never knew my father, but in my dreams he is brave and strong, like you." She drew back and studied him. "You're too young to be my father. Are you eighteen?"

"Sixteen. I was born near midsummer."

"Still, more like a father." They fell silent, and she laid her head against his shoulder.

AT FIRST I thought Sigurd was another enemy, and that I was about to die. Then he fought them, and I saw that he didn't look like them, with their dark hair and eyes, but like us, with blue eyes and blond hair. I will never forget his fierceness. He killed three men in a moment. The man holding Gerde got away only because Sigurd had an arrow through his leg.

I felt his fury during the fight. I was afraid because his eyes were wild and angry. Then he came to me and cut my ropes and treated me kindly. He looked like Afi except young and strong, and I knew I could trust him. Now he's like a father to me, the only family I have. I'm lucky to be alive. If he hadn't come I would be dead or stolen away like Gerde. I will always be grateful, but I hope I never see that anger in his eyes again.

I don't remember my parents. My father died before I was born and my mother shortly after. Gerde thought she remembered them, but she wasn't sure. They were both gone by her third birthday, and after that Amma and Afi took care of us. We loved our grandparents, but Afi never seemed like my father; he was too old and couldn't do much any more. Sigurd is what I dreamed my father would be like. In my heart I know he's a good man.

Sigurd killed a buck, and we have eaten well since. I tried to sing our thanks to the buck, and sorrow for his death, a song Amma had taught me, but I started crying and couldn't finish. It was evening, the time Amma always sang her songs of gratitude, and as I sat there sobbing, unable to sing, I saw tears in Sigurd's eyes too. He says I remind him of his sister, who died in a raid like the one on Fosser.

We stayed in that camp more than a month before Sigurd could walk comfortably. For all that time we had a good place by a stream. I tended his wounds, gathered firewood, built the fires, and did some of the cooking. I also watched fish in the stream and saw butterflies, and he taught me to hunt. Finally, when he was strong enough, we hiked down from the mountains to the coast and started north toward Fjellheim. I was farther from home than I had ever been. I've always loved seeing new places, and now every step was new.

On the first day along the coastal path, we met a friend of Sigurd's. "Vadi!" he said, and they embraced. Then Sigurd put his hands on my shoulders and brought me in front of him. "This is Inge, my daughter!"

I couldn't believe I had heard him say it. It gave me a thrill.

They talked for a long time about what had happened and about the raiders. Vadi and three friends were heading south toward Hvit Elv. Vadi said the raiders never attacked Hvit Elv, and I'm glad. I knew children there, children I saw born.

Vadi sat beside me. "Inge, you have a valiant warrior for a father. He is our leader, and we feared he was dead. I'll see you again in Fjellheim. Go to my wife, Otama, and tell her I love her. She will have a baby soon." Then he and his friends went on south, and Sigurd and I went north.

That night, before we slept, I told Sigurd he surprised me by saying I was his daughter.

"That's how you feel to me, even though you remind me of my sister. I've never had a daughter to love, and you've never had a father to love you and take care of you, so we need each other." His smile touched my heart.

I hurt when I think of Amma, Afi, and Gerde, all gone. But I'm not alone, and I can feel the workings of fate. I was destined to grow up under Sigurd's protection.

FOR THE FIRST HALFMONTH in the streamside campsite Sigurd rested, making arrows and talking to Inge. He cured the deer's sinew in the sun and used it for bowstring and binding for arrowheads. He staked the hide on the sunny rocks to cure, but one morning the hide was gone and wolf tracks were everywhere. He was more careful with the meat, building a drying rack over the fire by weaving branches Inge collected. He tired quickly and napped a great deal, although less as he recovered. He hunted as much as he could, and soon they had ample dried meat. Inge collected berries for their meals, and they ate well.

Inge spent some of that time drawing and painting on the rock wall along their gully. She drew people, animals, flowers, trees—whatever she needed to illustrate that day's story. Sigurd often came upon her softly singing an extended story about a painting, and each time it brought him face to face with the loss of his mother, whose songs formed many of his early memories. His years of not weeping for his family ended in those days camped with Inge.

A few days after they arrived, Sigurd woke from an afternoon nap and went looking for Inge. He found her sitting on a log downstream, painting with her fingers on the rock wall, using yellow and green paints she had made by mashing leaves with water in shallow dished rocks. She was glad to see him. "I was happy to find these plants, and I don't even know their names. Amma told me, but I forgot."

The painting covered two armspans of the wall. She had sketched it using charred sticks and was now applying green paint to the grass and trees. "The fire is the village burning. I have no red paint, so I used yellow and black. The black men are the raiders. The yellow ones are the people in the village. The man who caught me and tied me up smelled terrible, so I drew him as a stinkbeast." Sigurd had to look twice to see that the stinkbeast was dead, broken in half.

"I don't see you."

"Oh," she said happily, "I'm not there. Look up here—the green man rescued me. That's you." In the upper corner of the rock, a large green figure was flying above the scene, arms spread like the wings of an eagle. He held a small yellow figure by the hand.

INGE SUFFERED FROM NIGHTMARES at first. More than once, Sigurd woke her after hearing her whimper in her sleep. She wouldn't talk about her dreams, saying it was bad enough to experience them. Once she woke in wide-eyed terror and looked around in confusion. Then she focused on Sigurd and hugged him in desperate relief. "Oh! You're alive! Thank goodness." She wouldn't go on and was unwilling to sleep again that night. After that, Sigurd sat with her in the evening, and they talked until she drifted off to sleep. On those nights she rarely had nightmares.

They talked of many things in that month of forced isolation—of their families, their grief, their fond memories. "Amma and Afi always worried about what would happen to Gerde and me when they were gone," Inge said. "They would be pleased to know of you." She never spoke of the ache of not knowing what happened to her sister, and Sigurd never asked.

On a twilit midnight soon after they arrived, Sigurd sat suddenly upright, sensing that they were not alone. He always slept with his weapons within reach, and he came quickly to his feet, club in hand, but he saw nothing. Then two small animals crept out of the bushes toward the remains of the fire—puppies, four or five months old, thin as skeletons, drawn by the smell of roasting meat. They explored the fire until one of them touched a nose to a hot coal and drew back with a piercing yip. Inge was awake in an instant.

"*Puppies!*" she squealed, and then, "Ohh, you're *starving.*" She reached into the food sack and gave them two small chunks of venison. By the time the puppies had gobbled the food, she had one of them on her lap. "Don't eat too much too soon," she crooned. "It will make you sick." But she gave each of them another small piece. "Sigurd, I dreamed of them, and when I woke up, there they were! The black one is Bjorn. The one with the white is Lyna. I dreamed their names." The pups by this time were nose-to-nose with her, as happy with her as she was with them.

"They've probably been on their own since the raid," he said. "I'm surprised they survived, with no home."

"Well," she said firmly, "they have one now."

Sigurd's family had never kept dogs. Sigurd's father disliked them and never tired of pointing out how much they ate and what a mess they made. Sigurd felt a tinge of resentment over the food the pups would need, but when he looked at Inge sleeping in the moonlight with her two charges, the sweetness of the scene made his resentment feel selfish. That was the first time he saw her smile.

WHEN SIGURD HUNTED, Inge often walked with him, silent as a shadow. On an evening when they roasted and ate a rabbit she had spotted, she surprised him. "Sigurd, would you teach me to hunt?"

He gave her an appraising look. "You'd be a good hunter, with your sharp eyes and your understanding of animals. We'll start by making a bow light enough for you to draw. I'll show you how to make arrows and arrowheads—easy to do, if you're careful and work slowly. Accurate shooting is hard to teach, but I suspect you'll do well."

The next morning she was so excited about learning to shoot that she almost couldn't eat. They found a modest oak branch, straight and dry, and cut it to her arm span. Sigurd shaped it roughly, notched it, and strung it with a length of cured sinew. He gave her one of his own arrows to practice with. He drew a cross on a massive rotting oak log with a blackened stick and, from fifteen paces away, used the new bow to shoot an arrow almost exactly into the center of the cross. Inge was too excited at first to settle down and aim; she missed the log repeatedly, and searching for the arrow frustrated her each time. Once she had the idea, they increased the distance to thirty paces. She practiced until midmorning, when her fingers were too sore to draw the bow.

"Well, then," Sigurd said, "we can make arrows and arrowheads." They collected beech branchlets for arrows somewhat shorter than his. He showed her how to cut the slit to receive the arrowhead and attached one of his own with sinew. At the tail of the arrow, he cut the notch for the bowstring.

"What about the feathers?" She was holding one of his finished arrows, examining it closely.

"They make shooting more accurate, but adding them takes time. You'll break arrows at first, and lose them. Better to wait until you're over that before you add feathers. Making flint arrowheads takes time too. You can simply carve points on your practice arrows."

When Sigurd woke the next morning, Inge was nowhere in sight. He found her practicing at their oak-log target area, explaining everything she did to the puppies.

When she saw him, she leapt up in excitement. "I was awake before the sun, thinking about shooting. I came here as soon as I could see the log. Watch!"

She shot three successive arrows into the log from forty paces, all within a hand span of the cross. "You're good at it," Sigurd said. "I thought you would be. Do your fingers hurt?"

She showed him her right hand; two fingertips were bloody.

"Time to stop for the day. Your fingers will toughen soon enough." Walking back to camp, he added, "You'll be excellent. I've taught boys, but never a girl. And I never taught a boy who could shoot so well after one day."

Inge practiced every day, early in the morning. She soon wanted a stronger bow, and they sought out a stouter branch. She was making serviceable arrowheads by the time Sigurd was able to travel. The high point of her early archery career came on the day they left their camp. They were on the high ridge trail, walking in gathering dusk and seeking a camping place for the night, when she froze, holding her hands down to stop the dogs. Moving slowly, she took her bow from her shoulder, notched an arrow, and drew the bow. Sigurd didn't see what she was aiming at until a mortally wounded dark-colored rabbit leapt straight upward out of a shrub forty paces from them. Inge glowed with pride. "Even the dogs didn't know he was there."

MIDSUMMER WAS FAR BEHIND THEM now, and the nights were completely dark, at least briefly. Sigurd woke one night to find a northern lights show in progress, a beautiful fantasy scene, rare during the summer months. He glanced at Inge, curled up as usual with the puppies. She too was awake and looking at the sky.

"Amma took me outside to see the lights many times, for the strength they would give my spirit. She said fate would be kind to me in the end but that I might not live to adulthood without some terrible times. I had told her of a dream of what lay ahead, so awful that I had trouble sleeping. Now I feel safe."

She went quickly back to sleep, but Sigurd remained long awake. Inge's little-girl self reminded him painfully of Gudrun, and Inge's songs of gratitude and sorrow to her rabbit kills brought his mother to mind. Even the campsite stirred memories; at nine, hunting with his father, Sigurd had camped in a similar spot, with a stream and a pool. That time seemed impossibly far away now. As he lay there wracked by grief, overwhelmed by images of his family, Sigurd understood that caring for the little girl sleeping near him—simply taking on the everyday responsibility for a child—was bringing him back to life.

HAEFNIR LEARNED OF RAIDERS heading for Fosser and Hvit Elv two full days before the Fosser raid. He immediately headed south with eighty fighters. Vadi joined that group on the second day after he left Sigurd and Erland, and together they arrived in Hvit Elv before the raiders. There was no pitched battle; when the raiders found the village defended, they melted back toward Fosser. From there they continued upstream and left the area through the mountains as they had come.

Vadi returned to Kystenlandsbyen with Haefnir and thirty men, leaving fifty to guard Hvit Elv. Later in the summer, returning to Hvit Elv to call the rest of the fighters back, he encountered a lame man traveling north with a young girl and two puppies. He didn't recognize Sigurd until he saw him face to face.

"Sigurd! You're thin and limping, but you're alive! And who is this?"

"My daughter, Vadi! Inge, from Fosser!" Sigurd beamed with happiness. "She'll live in Fjellheim with me this winter. I can still barely walk, and it will be months before I'm strong enough to fight." He showed Vadi the broken arrow and the scars in his thigh. They camped together that night where they met. Vadi and Sigurd talked until midnight.

"We got to Hvit Elv in time to drive them off," Vadi said. "We followed them as far as Fosser but found no sign of you. What happened after I left?"

"Erland and I attacked four raiders who had captured Inge and her sister. Erland and three raiders died, and one escaped with Inge's sister. Inge and I fled for our lives. We camped for a month in a gully below the high ridge. After you left me, how long was it before you returned to Fosser?"

"I met Haefnir after a day and a half." Vadi counted days on his fingers. "Another day back to Hvit Elv. Fosser two days later. Five days total."

"Inge and I got to our mountain camp on the third day after the raid. The raiders looked for us actively for two full days. Maybe that's what saved Hvit Elv."

"I'm happy you're alive. And Haefnir will be delighted to see you."

SIGURD STILL MOVED SLOWLY, and after leaving Vadi he and Inge took four days to reach Kystenlandsbyen, where they stayed two nights. The bustle of a large town fascinated Inge, who knew only Fosser and Hvit Elv, tiny villages. She met the fighting men, who called her Sigurdsdottir.

In Fjellheim, summer had ended and a chill was in the air. Sigurd and Inge found Asah downstream from the village harvesting grain with her sons Oddi and Ragnar, along with Gunnar, now twelve, a good-looking boy, far different from the frail child Sigurd remembered from the Elvdal raid. Ragnar too had grown. At nine, he was big enough to help with the harvest.

Asah straightened up, saw Sigurd, Inge, and the dogs, and dropped her tools. "Oh! Sigurd! I was almost sure you were alive! But Vadi told me everything, and I was afraid too. I am glad to see you." She knelt in front of Inge. "And who is this beautiful child?"

"Asah, I lost much, but I gained a daughter. This is Inge, from Fosser. She's an accomplished healer, for nine—she helped me recover and made that time a happy one. Inge, this is Asah, the healer I told you about. She will help you learn."

"I'll be ten soon, at the equinox," Inge said, and Asah smiled.

Asah put her hands on Sigurd's shoulders, and the two regarded each other in silence. "I see you're a different man," she said. "Left a warrior and came back a father. When I foresaw your troubled summer, I didn't see Inge. This is the first time I've seen you look happy."

"He rescued me from raiders, Asah," Inge said. "He saved my life. He was shot in the leg doing it."

"Were the dogs your puppies?"

"They found us later. They were starving, but Sigurd had killed a deer, and we had plenty of meat. Now they're getting fat." One of the dogs was straying toward Asah's goat, which was cropping grass in the adjacent field. "*Bjorn!*" Inge shouted. "*Stop* that!" The dog scampered back to her side.

Gunnar and Asah's boys clustered around. Gunnar could not hold back his questions. "Sigurd, will you limp all your life? Will you show me where you got shot? Did it hurt?"

"Later, at home. Yes, it hurt, but Inge treated it, and I'll be fine in a few months." Sigurd turned to Inge. "This is Gunnar, and Asah's sons Oddi and Ragnar. Gunnar and I escaped from Elvdal together. Asah and Ragnar were there too, and after we met them Asah brought us here and gave us a home."

"He rescued me too," Ragnar said to Inge. "From wolves."

"Help us carry these loose stalks," Asah said, "and we can go to the house and eat." She turned back to Inge. "Welcome, Inge. This is a joyous day."

SIGURD IS BUILDING A HOUSE for us, close enough to Asah's that I will be able to visit her easily, even in winter. I will go every day if she will have me, to learn from her. She knows all the plants here, for medicine and dyes as well as food. When she saw Sigurd's arrow wounds, she asked me how I treated them. She nodded and smiled that I had known to use thyme. I told her Amma was a healer, and we talked about Asah's teacher—her mother. Asah is the only midwife in Fjellheim, and when I told her I helped Amma at many births, she laughed out loud. "I hope you'll help me too! It was a lucky day for me when you came here."

Otama and Vadi will live in the new house too. Vadi's family's house is already crowded, and with a new baby it would be difficult. Otama is already getting big; her baby—her first—is due before midwinter. She is young and beautiful, and she thinks Vadi is wonderful. She admires Sigurd as well, and when I told her how he had rescued me from raiders, her eyes opened wide. "I hope raiders never come here."

I hope that too.

For now, we live in Asah's house, which is a single large room, three armspans square, and crowded, especially with the dogs. They sleep with me, and Asah is good-natured about it, but I think she'll be happier when they leave.

Sigurd is building our house on the upstream side. It will have one room too, like all the houses here. Amma's house in Fosser had two, side by side, with a hearth in each one.

SIGURD IS STRONGER every month, and we go hunting often. We don't yet have nearly enough hides for the walls and floor of the house. Sewing the hides is a big job, but Asah says that once we have enough, the village women will help with the sewing while Sigurd and Vadi and others put the house up. Some families have more cured hides than they need and will lend us some so we can get the house up sooner. We already have the reeds we need for roof thatching. I have been going downstream with Gunnar to cut them. Sigurd is pleased with our progress and says we will have the house ready for winter unless we have an exceptionally early snow.

Asah is surprised that I have my own pouch. Her tradition is to save a girl's pouch for her until she comes of age at fourteen. Amma's was the same, but she gave me my pouch when I was six. She explained that she might not be there to give it to me when I needed it. I wonder—what did she foresee? Afi carved a beautiful little bear for my pouch, to keep me safe from bears, and Amma carved a pregnant mother with a big belly. When I have my own children, I will think of Amma.

I've learned more about Sigurd by talking to Otama. He is the strongest and fiercest warrior of them all, and the fighters look up to him as their leader. I can understand, because I will never forget the way he fought the raiders. I am thankful that he has become my father. Still, I'm happy to call him Sigurd, because I am his friend as well.

I am excited about the house and about painting pictures on the inside walls. I will have the yellows and blues and greens that Amma used, as her mother and grandmother did. Living in a house with Amma's colors will bring her back to life for me. I will start my paintings with the rescue.

WINTER CAME LATE; no snow had fallen by the festival of spirits, a month and a half before midwinter. Sigurd no longer limped, but he still tired easily. He spent many days hunting, usually with Inge or Gunnar. Between them, they killed, dressed, and brought back twelve deer before the festival of spirits.

Haefnir disbanded the fighting group in Kystenlandsbyen for the season, confident that raiders would never venture forth so late in the year, when they would risk being snowed in far from home. Vadi returned to Fjellheim to find the house-building project ready for his help. Otama, near her time, stitched hides, along with Inge, Asah, and two other women. Sigurd had leveled a flat space with holes for the six major posts. Preparing the wood took him almost a month. He selected and cut the six trees and trimmed them of branches and bark. He cut and trimmed almost two dozen substantial branches for the frame and braces, dragging them to the house site himself, and collected reeds for the roof and sticks for the walls, stacking them on the streambank.

With Vadi and two others, Sigurd dragged and rolled the six heavy trunks to the house site and notched them to receive their bracing. Using the village's single scaffold, the men erected the posts and tied the bracing into the notches with hide and sinew. Then Sigurd and Vadi built the walls, tying floor-to-ceiling sticks side by side, chinking them with mud and clay.

The house was Fjellheim's tenth and smallest, two armspans wide and three deep. Its single room had a cooking hearth in the center under a small smoke hole.

It took only five days to attach the sewn hides to the inside walls and lay thatch on the roof. The rear of the house had a packed dirt floor at first, because there weren't enough hides to cover the entire room, but the house was warm and dry. Sigurd dug a trench around it to keep water away.

Inge loved the house long before it was complete, and in its emptiness it gave the feeling that it was ready to begin a journey. Four people and two dogs moved in a month before midwinter, on a cold and blustery day that threatened snow. Asah arranged a feast of celebration the next day, held in the new house. Every family contributed food, and during the afternoon more than fifty people came. They all knew Inge by then, and her story; she felt welcome and lucky. And when

Otama's baby was born—a healthy boy, whom Otama named Kjell—Inge came into her own, helping with the birth and afterward.

The dogs slept with Inge at first, but when Kjell was born, protecting him became their life's mission, and they abandoned Inge's sleeping pallet for Otama's. They were still playful, although nearly full grown. They loved cold weather—they had dense, curly coats—and during daytime spent as much time outside as in. With three adults, a baby, a young girl, and two dogs, the house was a busy and cheerful place.

THE NEXT HALFMONTH included three severe storms, and by midwinter Fjellheim was isolated by deep snow. At the celebration of the midwinter moon, Asah presented Kjell to the village. The exertions of hunting and house-building had helped Sigurd recover completely, and when the weather turned clear and cold, he and Vadi enjoyed their first hunt of the winter.

"What will you do this spring?" Vadi asked. The two sat by their fire on the last night of a three-day hunt. They had killed a large doe and were tired, full of food, and satisfied with the trip.

"I will go to Kystenlandsbyen, at least this season. But raising a child has lessened my taste for battle, and I suspect this will be my last year. Fjellheim can use me as a hunter, and I will never again be as fast as I was."

"I feared you would not return at all. When you decide to be a father instead of a fighter, Haefnir and the men will regret it. Will Inge need care, while you're gone?"

"No. She's tough and independent, and she always does her share and more. She works so hard that I forget she's only ten. If she and Otama should need help, Asah is close, and Gunnar can help them too."

They were nearing sleep, lying on their backs under the stars, before Vadi spoke again. "How does it feel to have a daughter? I know she's not really your daughter, but she is changing you the same way a daughter would."

"Color has come back into my life. I told you long ago I didn't want to be one of those men who live for battle. Taking care of Inge, watching her recover from losing her family, makes the fire of battle seem unimportant. I had no idea what joy she would bring me. She's nearly grown, and this happy time won't last. But I want to enjoy it while it does."

"You could have your pick of women, you know. You could have children of your own."

"I have enough children, for now." Sigurd laughed— a laugh Vadi realized he had almost never heard. "But Inge will be lovely, and all too soon she will find some man her own age. When that happens—well, then I'll come to you for some of that advice."

"We all wondered what girl would finally bring down the hero Sigurd. It never occurred to us it would be a child."

SIGURD AND VADI hunted often after that, sometimes with Gunnar or Inge, whose skill with bow and arrow was the subject of much comment. The hides they brought back kept Inge and Otama busy stitching. When Sigurd was away and she wasn't sewing hide, Inge began sketching on the inside walls of the house. She would have no paints until summer—the dye plants were past their season.

As spring approached, Inge's thoughts of collecting dye plants faded and she grew anxious about Sigurd's impending departure for Kystenlandsbyen.

"I don't like it either," Sigurd said to her. "In the past, I left here in good conscience. No more." They had finished the last meal they would share. Sigurd and Vadi planned to leave the following morning.

"I'll miss you, but I'll be with friends. When will you return?"

"In earlier years I've stayed until the end of the season, after your birthday, but this year may be different. I have a daughter to take care of."

Inge smiled, but with tears in her eyes.

SIGURD'S DEPARTURE left me saddened. I lived in the house with Otama and baby Kjell, and the days passed slowly. I wasn't miserable, but I did miss Sigurd. I saw Asah every day. I helped her deliver six babies that spring. I walked with her to learn about plants, and this time I will remember them. She was kind, and I enjoyed her company, but I sometimes had nightmares and woke up wishing Sigurd were there to comfort me.

The cold spring gave me lots of fire-building practice. I collected wood in the forest in the afternoons and started a fire every morning. Afi rose early each morning to build the fire at home in Fosser. Thinking of him reminded me that he was gone and I was lucky to be alive.

The place before the hearth quickly became my favorite spot in our house, the place I went for comfort when I woke from a nightmare. It made the house feel like home. That same spot was there before the house was built, but outside then, with storm wind and deep snow. By enclosing it, the house made it seem a different place completely. That's the magic of a house. When I was six, in Fosser, our neighbor's house burned down. I had played in that house and knew it well. After the house burned I stood where I had played and wondered how a structure could be so important. Amma said it was a good question. Afi said questions like that were a waste of time.

LAST NIGHT I had a vivid dream I will never forget. Something immense and dangerous intended to kill me and eat me. I think it could fly, but that seems impossible, because it was as big as a house. It roared and stank. I could only catch glimpses. I thought I would surely die.

"A dragon," Asah said, when I told her of the dream. "How well it fits your life."

I wasn't sure what a dragon was. I must have looked completely puzzled. Asah laughed. "Inge, did your grandmother never tell you the story of the mighty Sigurd, who slew the terrible dragon Fafnir?"

Amma told Gerde and me many old tales, but I didn't remember a dragon, and I had not heard the name Sigurd before I met my Sigurd.

"I was very young. If she told me about Sigurd or a dragon, I must have been asleep."

"Sigurd surely heard the story from his mother. I heard it from my grandmother."

This conversation occurred early in the morning. I was helping Asah with a birth. The baby had not yet been born, and the mother was asleep. Asah and I were sharing a mug of tea.

"I'll tell you the story this evening," she said. "We have other responsibilities now."

I LOOKED FORWARD to that story all day. The morning birth resulted in Fjellheim's newest dweller, a healthy baby boy. I cooked dinner for Otama and left her and Kjell with a fine fire. Asah had built a fire too, and made tea. The three boys and I gathered around her as she told the story. Ragnar was excited to hear it, although she had told it several times before. The evening felt magical. I closed my eyes and let Asah draw me into the tale.

"This is the story of Sigurd and the dragon Fafnir," she began. "It begins with Sigurd's father. His name was Sigmund, and he was the mightiest of all warriors of that time. He had a magical longsword, Gram, that could never be conquered. Gram came from Odin himself! Odin dressed as an old one-eyed man and came into the hall of Sigmund's father, whose name was Völsung. Many people were there, eating and drinking. A huge tree grew in the center of that hall, and Odin drove the sword into the tree, up to the hilt. Then he turned and spoke to the crowd. 'This is the great sword Gram. None can wield it but the hero strong enough to draw it out.'

"Every guest tried to pull the sword from the tree, and every one failed. Then Völsung's son Sigmund gripped the sword. He was only fourteen, but he did what none of the others could—he pulled the sword from the tree. The sword was rightfully his, and he used it for many years.

"Sigmund took a wife named Hjordis, and the two of them lived together happily—until tragedy struck. Sigmund was in battle, wielding the sword and vanquishing every enemy, when he found himself facing an old man."

Ragnar jumped up excitedly. "Odin! In disguise!"

"You give away the story!" Asah exclaimed. "Remember, Inge has never heard it." Ragnar settled down, content.

"Yes! It was Odin! And he shattered the sword. Without it, Sigmund was helpless in battle, and his enemies overcame him.

"Hjordis ran to him in despair, and he spoke to her as he lay dying. 'Find the shards of the sword! Save them for our son, Sigurd.' This puzzled Hjordis, because they had no son. 'Tell me of Sigurd,' she said.

"'You shall bear our son, and he shall remake the sword and slay the dragon Fafnir.' Hjordis trembled when she heard this, for the dragon was a creature of the dark, an awful monster. But she never forgot what Sigmund said in his final moments."

Asah was a wonderful storyteller, far more exciting to hear than Amma. At the words "Slay the dragon Fafnir!" she jumped up in excitement. She spoke slowly with eyes wide when she said, "Yes, it was Odin!" I had never before heard her kind of storytelling.

"That very night, Hjordis went out onto the battlefield in the moonlight and collected the many fragments of the great sword Gram." (Here Asah stooped as she walked slowly through the room, looking in every corner.) "She carried them home and set them aside for her son, Sigmund's son Sigurd. As she did, she felt the first stirrings of life stir within her." (Asah's hands flew to her belly.)

"Mother," Ragnar said, "you left out about Sigmund's mother."

"I cannot tell the story all at once, Ragni. That part will have to wait for another time. Sigmund lived a long life, and when he died in battle, he was an old man. He had many adventures when he was younger, and other wives, and other children. But our story tonight is about his son Sigurd."

"Will you tell Inge all the stories?"

For myself, I like hearing stories a little at a time, because they are easier to remember that way.

Asah laughed. "Yes, I'll tell them all, but this one first. Well, Hjordis took the fragments of the sword and set them aside. After Sigurd was born,—"

A commotion outside interrupted Asah, and she opened the door to look out into the night.

"Sigurd! Vadi! What an unexpected delight! Come in! We have food!"

Sigurd and Vadi had come home for a short visit, something the Seacoast Guard allowed them once each year. They would stay only one night. I had not expected Sigurd. I had been hiding from myself how much I missed him, and it all came out in a rush of surprising tears.

"I was telling them the story of the hero Sigurd," Asah said, "and how he killed Fafnir the dragon. The rest of that story will have to wait."

SPRING PASSED INTO SUMMER, and eventually I had enough dye plants to begin painting the walls of our house. I remembered the painting I had made on the rocks in our camp, showing Sigurd rescuing me, and I began with a painting like that. I sketched it lightly in charred wood until I was happy with it. The night I put the first paint on it, I had a nightmare, the usual one— the village burning, people screaming, and the man binding me. Then I dreamed that Sigurd arrived and saved me from the nightmare, exactly as he had saved me from the raid itself. In my dream, he sat on my sleeping pallet and whispered to me, rubbed my shoulders to relax me, and told me we would hunt together the next day. I knew it was a dream, but still it comforted me, and I slept.

When I woke in the morning, the fire was already burning. Sigurd *had* come home! It had not been a dream!

"I am so glad to see you." I hugged him for a long time and cried. "I'm sorry to cry about something happy. I hate it when you're gone."

"I won't leave again. We fought a battle and beat the raiders badly, but my heart was here, and I realized I was through with fighting. As soon as we returned to Kystenlandsbyen after the battle, I told Haefnir that I have a young girl to take care of who needs me more than the fighters do. I said goodbye to the men, and here I am."

Asah had come into the house while he was talking. "I wondered how you could stay away. Vadi knows Otama will care for Kjell. You knew Inge was by herself. You no longer need to fight to follow your destiny. Now it lies here."

Sigurd brought news for Otama. "Vadi sends his love. He was a hero in the battle, and unhurt. I don't think the raiders will be back this year, and I doubt Vadi will stay in Kystenlandsbyen the entire season."

After that morning, everything changed for me. I started a garden with Asah and worked on my paintings every day. I hunted regularly with Sigurd. Time rushed by. Vadi did return earlier than usual, in late summer. He then worked alongside Sigurd and me to clear a new field for grain, downstream from the village. I sewed hides every evening, until we had enough to cover the entire floor. I had an ordinary home life for the first time since the raid on Fosser.

On the equinox, when I turned eleven, I realized that once again I was happy.

THE LIFE I LED in Fjellheim was a big change from Fosser, where I lived with grandparents and an older sister. I was now a working member of the household and the village. I helped Asah with every birth and helped Otama with Kjell. I fixed meals, made clothes for Sigurd and myself, dried meat, and helped plant and harvest grain.

Only a few events of that daily life stick in my memory. In the winter after I turned twelve, about the time Otama learned she was pregnant again, my monthly cycle began. Asah smiled when I told her that Amma had taught the motherless girls in Fosser how to deal with their own bodies as they grew up, and I went along with her on many of those visits. Now I didn't need teaching.

Otama was sick throughout that pregnancy. After Vadi left for Kystenlandsbyen in the spring, I took care of her as well as Kjell, and I was busy every day. Sigurd was busy too, helping to build a new house at the downstream end of the village, so a family there could have two houses instead of one that was terribly crowded. I helped sew the hides.

On a day when Sigurd was hunting, not working on the new house, a fire started somehow in the thatch that was ready for the roof, and a woman was badly burned trying to put it out. She never had a chance of recovering, but weakened and died, leaving her three young children motherless. Her husband did his best to care for them, but he needed help, and Asah and I both got to know those children well. By the equinox, the grieving husband had decided to move to Kystenlandsbyen, where his mother could help with the children. Sigurd and I went with him on that trip.

In Kystenlandsbyen, we talked to Vadi. "Nothing has been heard of the raiders for two and a half years," he said. "Maybe they're tired of losing so many men."

"Don't depend on that," Sigurd said, "but I doubt they'll attack so late in the season. Why don't you return with us?"

"Otama is near her time," I said. "She will need help."

"How could she need me, if she has you and Asah?" Vadi drew back and looked at me. "Inge, you've grown up while I've been away. You're much taller. Are you twelve now?"

"Thirteen. I've been in Fjellheim three years."

"A woman, almost." Then he laughed. "Every boy in Fjellheim must be thinking about you."

I felt myself blushing, because I realized how true his words were, about Gunnar in particular. He had been my friend since I arrived. Now I saw for the first time that he hoped for more. And that I had avoided thinking about marriage.

Vadi and Sigurd's talk turned to the raiders, and I wandered away to stare at the ocean and think.

As a child, I expected to marry and have a family when I grew up. Gerde and I even talked about what kind of men we wanted. Living with Sigurd, I put those ideas off to the side, because Fjellheim is tiny and has almost no boys my age. Besides, I wasn't grown up yet.

Now that has changed. I'll be fourteen soon. If I were living with Amma and Afi, they would hold a ritual ceremony of womanhood for me, with songs and a feast. Asah has said I will be a good wife and a good mother for my children, but until this moment that has seemed like the far future. I can still feel the terror of the raid when I remember it, and living as Sigurd's daughter soothes that wound. My life in Fjellheim feels fresh and new, and I'm not yet ready to go beyond it. But the idea of life with a husband isn't easy to dismiss either. Part of me wants it. Perhaps that's what Gunnar sees.

VADI WAS A CHEERFUL COMPANION on the walk back to Fjellheim. He and Sigurd talked about whether and when the raiders might next appear. Otama was excited to see him, and a halfmonth later I delivered their daughter Sefe, because Asah was delivering another baby. Amma would have been proud of me.

I added a painting of Vadi and Otama and their children to the walls, by now almost full of what I saw here and faces of the people I was close to. I hoped that someday my paintings might help Kjell and Sefe understand their village.

I continued to think about my future. After Vadi's light-hearted remark, I thought about love and marriage all the time, especially when Gunnar looked at me.

THE MILD WINTER gave way to an early spring. The last snow patches disappeared before the equinox, and wildflowers dotted the meadows. The warm sunshine drew older children outside, and doors and windows stood open throughout Fjellheim. Inge relished the added light as she surveyed her paintings. She had covered two walls and wanted to leave the others for Otama, who was still too busy to think about painting.

The late afternoon was hectic. Otama nursed Sefe while she fixed food for Kjell, now an active three-year-old, as he led the dogs through the house at high speed. Sigurd was hunting with Vadi and Gunnar. They were due back by evening, and Inge watched for them through the open door.

The sound of voices drew her outside, where she saw Sigurd talking urgently to four men. Inge recognized Haefnir, whom she had met in Kystenlandsbyen. Vadi had planned to go there within days, but it seemed that Kystenlandsbyen had come to him.

Sigurd and Vadi came into the house together, carrying most of a small doe they had killed, but they quickly put down their packs and hunting gear.

Inge saw the news in Sigurd's eyes before he spoke. "Our three years of peace is ended. The headland watch saw fifty raiders cross the river and walk westward. Haefnir suspects they might pass through Elvdal and come up its canyon. That would bring them here. Haefnir sent fifty men to follow the raiders, more than a day behind. Seventy more are coming here. They'll arrive soon and then continue up the canyon. Haefnir hopes to trap the raiders between the two groups."

Sigurd looked at Inge, and she knew what he would say next. "Vadi and I will join them, and we'll take Gunnar. We shouldn't be long. We'll meet the raiders far upstream, tomorrow night or the morning after." As he spoke, he stuffed arrows and his fighting knife into his pack and then strapped on his club and shield, unused for three years.

"Gunnar is no warrior," Inge said.

"He can help in many ways. We won't use him in the fighting. Think how he would feel if he stayed here."

Otama spoke quietly to Vadi. "I had planned to go with you to Kystenlandsbyen, to show off Sefe."

Vadi nodded toward the group outside the doorway. "Haefnir is too old to fight; he came this far only to persuade Sigurd to lead the men. He is going back to Kystenlandsbyen, and you can go with him. I'll join you in a few days. Fifty raiders will face more than a hundred of us. We think this battle will be quick."

Inge went again to the door and saw dozens of men in battle gear. More arrived as she watched.

Sigurd put his hands on Inge's shoulders. "Don't worry. I'll be back quickly." He and Vadi walked to the forming group, Gunnar joining them from Asah's house. Inge heard calls of, "Sigurd is coming!" and saw Sigurd in close conversation with Haefnir. Then the large group of fighting men followed Sigurd upstream and passed out of sight.

WALKING UP THE CANYON by the light of the moon, Sigurd realized that three years' respite had not made the prospect of battle more appealing. He was a householder now, a family man with a thirteen-year-old girl to provide for, almost the age he was in his first battle. He was dead inside then, truly living only when fighting. Raising a young girl for four years had restored him, and in his caring about Inge it horrified him to think of leaving her alone, bereft of still another family.

Sigurd's men hiked until late evening and rose the next day to the prospect of more. They walked through the morning and into the afternoon, nearing the high pass Sigurd remembered from his flight from Elvdal. In that time they saw nothing of the raiders. As the sun dropped lower, Sigurd began to doubt Haefnir's guess about the raiders' plan, and it came as a surprise when the raiders appeared after all.

The first contact occurred during a rest. Sigurd heard shouting from far ahead and knew raiders had spotted his fighters. He spread his men across the canyon, putting some along the walls, where they could be effective with bow and arrow. A few raiders appeared, trying to find a way around on the north side of the canyon, but they lost half their number to the archers, and Sigurd saw the survivors scramble back toward their main body. He ordered his men forward, and they advanced slowly on the raiders during the course of the afternoon. By dusk they had made no further contact.

Shouting erupted again as darkness fell, and a large group of raiders appeared, charging toward Sigurd's fighters, now arranged in an unbroken line across the canyon to keep the raiders from breaking through. Then Sigurd heard the sounds of fighting from the rear of the raider group; Haefnir's men were attacking. Sigurd's fighters surged up the canyon into the fray. Shouting was continuous, with occasional panicked screaming. Enough light remained for archery, and men on both sides fell, but the battle was one-sided, and its most intense phase was short. The raiders were caught between two superior forces.

Haefnir's fighters did not take prisoners.

SIGURD WALKED THROUGH THE BATTLEFIELD after the fighting ended. The ground was littered with dark-haired raider bodies—and seven bodies of the Seacoast Guard; even in the near dark, the blond fighters were easy to identify. Sigurd enlisted Vadi's aid to gather the seven bodies. He and his men camped nearby, with a guard and a fire to protect the bodies from wolves.

The night was overcast and dark. Sigurd rose at first light and roused Vadi and Gunnar, and the three of them started back toward Fjellheim. Sigurd hurried; he was uneasy. Rain stirred up mud and slowed their progress, and Sigurd's unrest grew as the morning wore on.

In midmorning they saw Tormod, a Fjellheim boy of eleven, running to meet them. He was red-faced with exhaustion and panic.

"Fires in Fjellheim." He gasped for breath. "Raiders came."

SIGURD AND VADI exchanged a grim look. "Some must have escaped us," Vadi said. Without a further word they both started running. Gunnar tried to run with them, but he could not keep up and soon dropped to a trot.

A broad pall of grey smoke hung over the village. As Sigurd and Vadi rounded the last bend in the stream, they saw nothing moving. Three houses were burned, including Sigurd's and Asah's. The sight of bodies on the ground numbed Sigurd, and in his shock he was thirteen again, entering the ruins of Elvdal with Gunnar. He moved mechanically toward the houses, not yet accepting the reality of what he saw.

The posts of his house still stood, surrounded by the smoldering remains of the hide walls. Nearby lay the bodies of three raiders. Beneath one was a crumpled form so covered in mud and blood that Sigurd couldn't see who it was. In his heart, though, he already knew, and when he rolled the lifeless body of the raider away from Inge, he saw her bow beneath her.

Sigurd collapsed to his knees, and icy horror closed in on him.

He turned Inge over. Mired in memories of Elvdal, he half expected his sister's lifeless face, but the agony of recognition pulled him into the present. He scooped Inge's limp body into his arms and cradled her against him. His images from the Elvdal raid, all the more potent after six years of aging, washed away in a flood of memories of Inge. Her terror when her sister was carried away; her tending his wounds; her determination to learn to shoot, her pride in her skill, her songs, paintings, caring. Her courage.

And a memory he could not face.

Near the end of their month in camp, Inge told him she had given up too easily, hardly fought the raiders. "I was afraid to make them so angry they would kill us both."

"Inge, you're a little girl. And you were unarmed. You had no choice. If your bow-and-arrow skill had been what it is now, you would have done better to fight to the death than succumb to barbaric treatment."

"When you fought, I could see you would never give up. I learned from you. If there is another time, I will not forget."

Sigurd could bear no further thoughts of the living Inge. He lowered his face to hers in despair.

AS HE GRIEVED, Sigurd realized Inge was breathing— bloody and unconscious but alive.

Asah approached with Ragnar, and Sigurd looked up at her. "She's alive. I don't see a wound, but I can't rouse her. I'm afraid for her." He carried Inge to the streambank. "Asah, there are hides in my pack." He shrugged off his pack and sank down onto the new grass, still cradling Inge.

Asah soaked a soft hide in the stream and cleansed Inge's face. "Ragnar and I were returning from the fields when people ran toward us, escaping. There were only a few raiders. I hope not many from the village died."

Sigurd sat on the grass beside the stream, cleaning Inge's neck and arms with a wet hide, his face a mask of fear. Asah looked down at her. "Sigurd, you must not give up hope. I think she will recover."

Vadi knelt by Sigurd. He held out three arrows. "Are these Inge's?"

"Those two are. This one I made. Where did you find them?"

"She killed three raiders, I think."

SIGURD RETURNED TO STROKING Inge's face and cleaning off sticky caked mud, and blood for which he still found no explanation. He dipped the hide in the stream and washed her face again.

He was rinsing mud from her hair when she opened her eyes.

"Oh—" She looked around in confusion. "Oh— Sigurd—"

She broke into tears. "You're alive. When I saw the raiders—"

She lay in Sigurd's arms, collecting her wits, trying to understand. She turned her head and saw their house, burned to posts. Only the evening before, the walls had held the paintings she worked on for three years.

She looked back at Sigurd, and he was astonished to see a smile spread across her face. She opened her arms wide, reached around his neck, and pulled herself up to him.

They remained that way, close in each other's arms, overcome by relief. The others walked away, reluctant to intrude.

HE WAS MY HERO from the moment he saved me.

In Fjellheim I woke every day happy to live with this man who adopted me as his daughter, happy to learn from him. He said it first—I've never had a daughter to love, and you've never had a father to love you, so we need each other.

You can come to depend on something a little at a time and not realize its importance until it is snatched away. I had a premonition when Sigurd went up the canyon to fight the raiders. He was away two nights, and I was full of anxiety. The second night I didn't sleep, and it came to me that I did not want any other husband, not Gunnar or anyone else. I wanted Sigurd to be my husband. I know he's almost seven years older. I know he has always loved me as a daughter, and maybe even as a little sister. But I also know we are good companions and could make each other happy as husband and wife.

After living with Sigurd, how could I be happy with anyone else?

IN THE MORNING I heard screaming and knew raiders had come to Fjellheim and were burning houses and killing. I thought it meant Sigurd was dead—that I had realized too late what I wanted, that I had lost him at the same moment I recognized he was the only man for me. I could not face that. I no longer cared whether I lived or died. I didn't care about the house burning. I shot the three men with no feeling of triumph or revenge; I did it because otherwise they would have killed everyone and burned the entire village. But still I thought I was too late.

Then I woke up in Sigurd's arms. I thought I might be dreaming, but when I saw Asah and the burned house, I knew he had returned alive.

Not too late.

I would not let that opportunity escape. I pulled myself up to him and said, in the fiercest voice I could find, that I never ever wanted to be separated from him again as long as I lived, and that I wanted him to be my husband, if he would.

I saw his answer in his eyes. The possibility had been before us all along, but invisible, because in our minds we had remained the nine-year-old girl and the sixteen-year-old warrior who saved her and took her on as a daughter.

Sigurd drew me close. "When I thought you were dead, I wondered how my life could mean anything without you. How could I love anyone else?"

17

ASAH RETURNED to find Sigurd and Inge as she had left them, clutched together, now murmuring to each other, soft things Asah couldn't hear. She sat to wait.

Inge looked at her. "You knew all along we would marry, didn't you?" She was still in Sigurd's arms. Both were smiling.

"Inge, I saw it from the day I met you. I see it now in your happy faces." Asah looked around at the morning's aftermath. "But your paintings! Like a death."

Inge surveyed the destruction. "The house and the paintings mean nothing compared to what we have discovered."

"Asah," Sigurd asked, "will you marry us?"

"I will, in three days, in Kystenlandsbyen. My sons and I will go there today and for now will live with my brother's wife's family. At the equinox, I will say the prayers for those we have lost. Then I will marry you, and you can be on your way."

"You saw that we will leave?"

"Since the day Inge came here, I have seen the two of you with your children and grandchildren, living in peace. That can't happen here. But will you be happy by yourselves? Where will you go?"

Sigurd looked down at Inge, still in his arms. "We've been talking about that. After the raid in Fosser, we were alone for more than a month while I recovered, and we both remember that time fondly, despite the events that led to it. In Hvit Elv they say the coastline to the south has no villages, as far as anyone there has gone. If we set out that way we would have all season to find a place to winter, perhaps in a cave. We want a place to raise our children that is free of the terror we've always known."

"In my dreams," Asah said, "I have seen you far south of here, with a family, and not alone. Perhaps you will settle in a village."

Vadi now stood beside them. "Fjellheim will be the poorer for your departure, and I will miss both of you, but in your shoes I too would leave. Even though I was born here."

EIGHT VILLAGERS lay dead.

Six raiders had reached Fjellheim. They came upon a family and killed them all, but the village's other women and children fled to safety. A group of older men banded together and gave their lives to kill three raiders.

The three surviving raiders threw burning torches onto the roof of Sigurd's house. Inge stood in the doorway and shot down all three, one by one. The nearest grabbed her and smashed her to the ground before he collapsed across her body. The blood on her was almost totally his, although she did have a bloody nose.

THOSE WHO HAD RUN DOWNSTREAM to escape the raiders began to filter back, and the fighters—both forces combined, more than a hundred men—returned from the upstream battlefield, bearing the bodies of their seven comrades. They found Sigurd and Inge sitting beside the stream waiting for them.

That afternoon the lost fighters and villagers were buried in Fjellheim. Asah and Inge joined to sing the prayers for the dead.

The raider bodies were buried in a common grave. At the battleground, the fighters had left the bodies of the raiders to the vultures.

ASAH BEGAN by singing. She stood on the bluff in the growing darkness, with the rising moon behind her. The fighting men sat in a half circle around her; the families of the Kystenlandsbyen men sat with them. The crowd was over two hundred all told. Sigurd and Inge sat with Vadi and his family, near Asah's sons and Gunnar.

Asah sang the ancient songs of sorrow for the eight villagers who had died in Fjellheim and the seven fighting men lost in battle. She spoke about each one. The people stood to sing together in the moonlight and then fell silent, heads bowed, as they thought of those who had died.

ASAH BROKE THE SILENCE. "We will now speak of the living." She led Sigurd and Inge forward, turned them to face the crowd, and placed evergreen crowns on their heads. "The spring is too young for a flower-strewn path, but we have done our best." An expectant murmur broke out.

The two made a striking couple as they stood together, and people talked about them for years afterward—Sigurd the hero warrior, broad and powerful, Inge slender and nearly a head shorter, looking like a sprite from the land of fairy people.

With her hands on Sigurd's and Inge's shoulders, Asah sang the ritual of the wedding ceremony, a song everyone had heard many times. At last all understood, and excited chatter broke out.

Asah bent to light a torch and walked to one side, where she had laid a pile of branches. She turned to the crowd. "I have been part of their tale since before they met. It began in fire." She lowered the torch and ignited the branches.

"Elvdal died in fire, and Sigurd's family and much of mine with it. Sigurd and I were each away from Elvdal, a stroke of fate. We met when he heroically saved my son Ragnar from wolves." The crowd was spellbound; not many had known.

The fire grew and crackled as Asah went on. "That was the first fire. I brought Sigurd home to Fjellheim, both of us grieving. At fourteen he came here to Kystenlandsbyen as a fighter and became your hero as well as mine."

The torch in her hand flickered as she walked around Sigurd and Inge to a second pile of branches.

"Inge grew up in Fosser, in the mountains above Hvit Elv. Fosser too died in fire." She torched the branches. "Inge's family was lost then. Inge was only nine and would have been lost too but for Sigurd. He was sixteen." All knew the story of the rescue.

"That was the second fire." Asah returned to stand with Sigurd and Inge, between the two blazes.

"Sigurd brought Inge to Fjellheim and raised her as his daughter—built a house and provided for her as she grew into this beautiful young woman." The evening was fully dark now, the moon large and brilliant behind the two fires.

"Then came the third fire—the raid on Fjellheim."

Asah stepped four paces toward the crowd and lowered the torch into a trench full of dry twigs and branches; Vadi and Gunnar had helped her prepare it. Fire sprang up as she followed the trench, and before the crowd realized what was happening, Asah, Sigurd, and Inge stood within a ring of fire.

The two larger bonfires, farther back along the bluff, were at their peak, and Asah had to raise her voice to be heard. "Most of us know the story of the fearless warrior who slew the dragon Fafnir—Sigurd, the great hero of the old tales. That story does not end with the death of the dragon. To win the love of Brynhild, Sigurd must enter a ring of magic fire. Brynhild! Warrior maiden, favorite child of Odin himself. And who raised that ring of fire? Yes! Loki! God of Fire!"

The crowd was rapt, dead silent.

"But for Inge, Fjellheim would have died as Elvdal and Fosser did. She is the only woman among us who has fought the raiders." Asah put her hands on Sigurd's and Inge's shoulders. "Now our Sigurd will wed his own warrior maiden in this ring of fire."

The crowd erupted into cheering and chatter, and Asah waited for silence.

"The fires to the left and right represent Sigurd and Inge. But it was the raid in Fjellheim that brought them together for life and brought them before you to marry. The ring of fire—Loki's magic fire, which shields all within it from harm—represents their love, and it is right that they stand within it. How could these warrior heroes find happiness except in each other's arms? Three days ago in Fjellheim each thought the other was lost. That agony has turned to joy, and tonight we are honored to witness their wedding."

Asah drew Sigurd and Inge to her within the ring, and firelight bathed them all as she clasped their hands between her own. Tears streamed down her face as Sigurd and Inge spoke the ancient promises. When Asah declared them husband and wife, few eyes were dry.

One further surprise: On a signal from Haefnir, the fighting men rose as a body, every man with a torch. They lit the torches from the flaming trench, and the men formed a long row of arches with more than a hundred torches overhead. As the wedded pair walked that aisle, the silence gave way to cheering that grew to a roar.

THEY SET OUT SOUTHWARD by moonlight with the sound of many farewells in their ears and hearts. Sigurd had prepared their packs in advance, with food from Vadi and Otama, and a packet of seeds, Asah's gift. By midnight, with the moon high, they found themselves on a bluff above the coast. Sigurd made up their sleeping pallet, the first they had ever shared. He built a fire, and until the birds sang they lay beside it and talked about the path before them.

EPILOGUE

"AUNT INGE?"

I open my eyes to see our daughter-in-law Alys with Yrsa, her first. Alys has always called me Aunt Inge, as her mother does, originally because Alys's grandmother and I thought of each other as sisters.

Yrsa reaches for me and laughs. She's only nine months old, but she and I have a special understanding—her wise old spirit accepts mine as an equal. Finally, in my last years, I have a granddaughter to love and teach as I was loved and taught. I will be learning from her as well, for she is quite extraordinary. Yrsa will become our spiritual leader. She is fascinated by fire, and it seems to flare in her presence. She is a creature of fire, this descendant of the Fjellheim raid.

I sit up and take her into my arms. She squirms off my lap onto our sleeping pallet to climb on Sigurd, who pretends to sleep. We recently discovered the luxury of afternoon naps, one of the privileges of old age. Today we are in Kyle and Alys's house in the village.

Alys has news. "Audun was hunting with Kyle. He ran home by himself to tell us travelers are coming here to see you and Uncle Sigurd." Audun is Yrsa's cousin, a boy of nine.

Sigurd is awake in an instant, of course; the warrior in him never sleeps, even at his age.

"Who?" He sits up, and Yrsa scrambles quickly onto his lap.

"Three men. They'll be here soon."

Yrsa's beauty takes my breath away. She has dark curly hair like Alys's mother, Ana, but bright blue eyes from Alys's father, Olaf, a northerner like us. Yrsa is somehow both delicate and robust. Sigurd stands and lifts her, and she sits on his arm, utterly satisfied with her lot. His first granddaughter, she has melted his heart from the beginning. Seeing them together reminds me of how kind he was to me when I first knew him.

Kyle's voice comes from outside. "Mother? People are here to see you."

Blinking in the sunlight, we emerge from the house onto the path from the river. None of the men is young. One might be sixty. His face is familiar.

Sigurd looks puzzled briefly and then breaks into a happy laugh. "Vadi!"

They are in each other's arms in an instant.

WE EAT WELL WITH OUR VISITORS—lamb that Kyle slaughtered yesterday and green vegetables from the garden by the river. The two younger men are Vadi's son Kjell, now over forty, and Asah's son Ragnar, over fifty.

Vadi is sixty-three. Working and hunting have kept him strong and healthy, although he is slowed and stiffened by age. "I am surprised to find I have lived so long. I am the oldest man I know."

Kjell is charming. "My first memory is of your wedding—of you and Sigurd in the ring of fire with Asah. People talked about that ceremony for years."

I remember Kjell that night too. He was three. I had helped with his birth, and he was the first baby I ever lived with. He has the same sweet nature and happy smile now.

"When Vadi decided to try to find you," Ragnar says, "I had to come. I'm happy you're both strong and healthy. So many people die young. Especially heroes." He glances at Sigurd.

The three men sailed from Kystenlandsbyen to Rivermouth in twelve days and walked here in five more. "I've wanted to come for years," Vadi says, "ever since we first heard about your victory over the raiders, not long after you left us. When I turned sixty I realized I must not put it off any longer."

"How did you hear about our battle?" Sigurd sounds surprised.

"How could we not? Every boat from the south brought word that the raiders had been completely destroyed. And that a man named Sigurd was one of the heroes. It had to be you. We've heard occasional news of you since then as well. That's how we knew how to find you."

"The raiders never recovered," Ragnar says. "They had already lost so many men near Kystenlandsbyen that they stopped coming that way. Instead, they went down the mainland coast, with huge numbers. Then their biggest group never returned—because of you. That was too much for them. They quit the area completely."

"We kept a fighting force in Kystenlandsbyen for five years," Vadi says. "Then Haefnir died, and it disintegrated."

"The Seacoast Guard was too much for the raiders," Sigurd says. "It kept that coast safe."

"Vadi," I say, "Tell us of Otama and Asah and your family."

"Asah lived until a few years ago. She talked about the two of you her whole life. Otama died young, in childbirth, when Sefe was three. Sefe still lives in Fjellheim."

"I'm saddened to hear about Asah. But Vadi, Otama's early death shocks me. That must have been hard for you, with two small children. Did you marry again?"

"Never. I lived with Asah, and she helped raise the children."

"Does Sefe have children?"

"Between her children and Kjell's, I have seven living grandchildren. And a new great-grandson."

"And Gunnar?"

"He died years ago, but two of his three sons are still alive. They also live in Fjellheim, which now has two hundred people."

Vadi looks around. "We expected your village to be bigger."

I laugh. "Oh, we don't live here. Come with me. I'll show you." I lead the three of them to the river road and then upstream until we can see the Benchland high above, at the top of the long, steep cliff that has protected us for nearly forty years.

I point to the clifftop. "Up there is where we live, with many others. Two of our children live down here, and four grandchildren. Our other children live up above. You won't need to climb that cliff to get there. We have an easier way, through a cave."

WHEN OLD WARRIORS GET TOGETHER, they talk of battles past and of other old warriors. Two nights later, our entire group gathers on the Benchland—more than fifty people. We sit by the fire at the outside shelters as Sigurd and Vadi laugh together and talk about fighting raiders. Vadi regales the group with tales of Sigurd's heroism. "I would be long dead but for him. I had an arrow through my leg and was unconscious on the ground. Sigurd clubbed raiders right and left to save me. His reward was an arrow in the shoulder. That was his first battle. He was fifteen."

"He saved me too," Ragnar says. "I was six. Wolves chased me and would have had me but for him. I think he was thirteen. That's why I came on this trip."

Everyone here knows how Sigurd rescued me, of course, because I painted it on the walls of our cave. Earlier today Sigurd and I showed our guests the cave and the paintings. Vadi's eyes were wide. "Inge, I remember your paintings in our house in Fjellheim. It was sad when they burned, but you have replaced them many times over, and these will be here as long as this cave remains."

When Sigurd led Vadi and the others outside, I stayed behind looking at the paintings, seeing them afresh through the eyes of our visitors. I stood before the first scene I painted, showing Sigurd and me standing with Asah in the ring of fire, and our long love came to my mind as a miracle of spirit. Years ago, Yrsa—my teacher and friend, the great healer for whom our granddaughter is named—told me that the love Sigurd and I share is no accident of fate, but ancient and eternal. It drew him to me, led to his rescuing me from raiders, and has held us together for life.

I moved on to look once more at my painting of Fjellheim burning on the day I feared he was dead. That was the day I knew he was all I ever wanted.

Part Two

Child of Fire

Authors' note

TWO DIFFERENT CHARACTERS in *Child of Fire* have the name Alys—one ancient, one modern.

In *Inheritance*, the ancient Alys and Jarrett Eriksson dream of each other and hear each other's names. Subsequently she refers to him as "Jered" and he to her as "Alice." The modern Alys plays only a fleeting role in that story.

Both women are major characters in *Child of Fire*. The modern Alys is "Alys" to all. The ancient Alys, however, is "Alys" to her contemporaries but "Alice" to Jarrett.

Two women with the same name. One of them with two different spellings. Why would we have seeded such confusion?

We had our reasons, as you'll see.

Fifty years after the fire wedding . . .

PROPHESY

THE TWO VOICES blend in the hypnotic rhythms of a song of prayer. The women look alike, with dark curly hair and dark eyes. They face a fire; behind them stands a throng of people of all ages. The cool clear midnight twilight is brightened by the full moon.

When the prayer concludes, the two stand silently facing the moon. After a time, they turn to the group. The younger woman leaves her mother to join a blond man and three small children. The crowd sits.

The older woman walks slowly, but her voice is strong and clear. "Overhead is the full moon of midsummer, and we gather to remember our history and speak of the future." Two men thump a hollow log in a repetitive rhythm. The sound is quiet and muffled, eerie in the night, and young children cling to their mothers.

"Forty-seven winters ago they came to the Benchland, our four founders—Zoan and Quitana, my parents, and Sigurd and Inge, parents of Kyle, Alys's husband. They were drawn here by the spirit of this place, the spirit that sustains us. We live in its embrace. It protects us and comforts us and shows us the way

forward." She stands with eyes closed, her body swaying slightly, and her speech falls naturally into the rhythm of the log drum. She has heard these ceremonies all her life. In recent years, she has been the speaker. She is Ana, the group's spiritual leader, its woman of wisdom.

"I loved them, all four. I heard them speak at the festival of the midsummer moon, and as a child I sat on their laps and heard their stories. Now they are gone, and it falls to me to speak for them." Something in her voice catches everyone's attention. A pulse of anticipation ripples through the crowd, almost fear. The drumbeat quickens.

"We have lived here in peace all that time, because our founders fought for us, but largely because our Benchland is beyond the reach of enemies. Now some of us live off the Benchland in houses near the river. Uncle Sigurd disapproved, because he came to manhood in a time of barbarian raids and thought our village below too exposed.

"We owe much to Uncle Sigurd. We live here because he wanted to have a secure place for us to grow. He never changed that view. Preparing for this evening, seeking guidance in the spirit chamber, I dreamed of the last thing he said to me. It is those words I must pass on to you.

"They will return, and the time is not far off. You must prepare to defend the houses near the river."

TRIP JOURNAL, Sunday July 1, 12:24 AM—I know all about clustering: nothing ever happens in isolation. Even so, I'm having trouble coming to terms with what happened today.

I'm camping in my truck after spending the day preparing for a one-day cave shoot tomorrow. I was in and out of the cave many times, setting up cameras and flash units and making test shots. I checked email every time I was outside, and I took part in two separate email exchanges from different parts of the world—on the same subject. What's *that* about?

It's past midnight, and I have to be ready at seven when the caving party arrives, but with today's emails on my mind, I can't sleep.

From: kramnick@johnshopkins.edu
To: jarrett@erikssonphoto.com
Date: Sat Jun 30 10:11 AM EDT
Subj: Alice's Cave

Jarrett - hi from me & Roger. We need to talk, said the girl. I've been working again on your photos of the tablet paintings from Alice's Cave. Weird results are making me nuts. Too complex for email. Do you have Skype?

From: jarrett@erikssonphoto.com
To: kramnick@johnshopkins.edu
Date: Sat Jun 30 10:45 AM EDT
Subj: Re: Alice's Cave

Hi, Mira—Sorry, no Skype. I'm in New Hampshire on a job, have phone & iPad, but terrible signal. Home tomorrow night. Try me by email, so I don't die of curiosity overnight. .../J

From: kramnick@johnshopkins.edu
To: jarrett@erikssonphoto.com
Date: Sat Jun 30 10:49 AM EDT
Subj: Re: Alice's Cave

You remember the upper entrance? Roger says you and he didn't go there but saw it on the cave map painted on the wall in the living chamber. I've been working with a three-panel tablet. Top left, head of a woman, Alice's mother. Top right, an overview map showing the upper entrance. I really didn't know what the tablet showed before now, because the paint had crazed, and until I figured out a way to see through the crazing, I saw only a scratch maze.

The bottom half of the tablet is a sketch of the upper entrance. And of ME. The drawing is quite clear. I'm wearing caving gear. What could THAT mean? I've never BEEN to the upper entrance.

Call us on Skype when you get home. There's more.

From: jarrett@erikssonphoto.com
To: kramnick@johnshopkins.edu
Date: Sat Jun 30 11:45 AM EDT
Subj: Re: Alice's Cave

I knew about the upper entrance. Re picture of you: Are you sure?

Call you late tomorrow night. .../J

MIRA'S EMAILS throw my mind out of sync by five thousand years. Alice's Cave is in Sweden. It's amazing—a big beautiful cave accessible only from an isolated shelf of land that itself is very hard to reach. The paintings Mira mentioned were made there during the Copper Age.

Alice's Cave was the focus of the longest cave expedition of my career. I spent three months there with Mira and Roger, her husband, both scientists as well as expert cavers. She's an anthropologist specializing in prehistoric human cultures, and the samples and photographs we brought back from Alice's Cave have served her well. She returns to studying them whenever her busy schedule permits, and she says she continues to be amazed by the flow of fresh findings from our expedition.

I thought I had put Alice's Cave behind me. I don't dream of it as often as I once did. My experiences there made me question my sanity, and I'm not sure I want to stir those demons again. Perhaps Mira and Roger will have to figure out this new mystery without me.

THE EXCHANGE WITH MIRA is the first part of today's story. Here's the second:

> **From: engberg@stockholmonline.net**
> **To: jarrett@erikssonphoto.com**
> **Date: Sat Jun 30 1:18 PM EDT**
> **Subj: Alice's Cave**
>
> Mr. Eriksson - I'm Alys Engberg. We met five years ago when you kindly agreed to lead a tour through Alice's Cave. I was then Sweden's Minister of Culture. We laughed together because we had beat-up old caving helmets and the rest of our group looked as clean as Christmas morning.
>
> Disturbing things have happened to me recently in Alice's Cave. I'm writing for moral support. Perhaps I'm hoping you can reassure me that I'm not losing my mind. Are you available by phone?
>
> Regards - Alys
>
> **From: jarrett@erikssonphoto.com**
> **To: engberg@stockholmonline.net**
> **Date: Sat Jun 30 3:01 PM EDT**
> **Subj: Re: Alice's Cave**
>
> Alys!! Of course I remember you. I'm on a cave shoot and won't be back in the land of phones until late tomorrow night. Can I call you Monday?

Whatever strange things happened to you in Alice's Cave, I can assure you that stranger ones happened to me, and that if you are losing your mind, I am too. It is a place of spirit power, and it wields a club over my mind.

I can't wait. Tell me what happened. When is a good time to call?

Jarrett

From: engberg@stockholmonline.net
To: jarrett@erikssonphoto.com
Date: Sat Jun 30 3:18 PM EDT
Subj: Re: Alice's Cave

Jarrett - Your email relieves my mind. I'll give you the outline now. I'll be in the air Monday. But for the rest of the week I'll be in the US, in DC. Can we possibly meet? I am committed Tuesday and Thursday, but Wednesday and Friday are free. I'm booked to return Saturday, but if you're not available this week, I'll rebook and meet you later at your convenience.

Alice's Cave is not much visited now. The current Minister feels we did everything necessary to protect it and sees no need for more. I fear he's not interested.

This is not true for me. Alice's Cave has come to dominate my thoughts. Your book usually lies open on my coffee table, and I have dreamed of the spirit chamber many times. I visited the cave alone a few times when I still had legitimate access.

Did you know of the upper entrance? I found it on the remarkable cave map in the living chamber and later spotted the entrance itself from outside. I would never have recognized it as an entrance if I didn't know; from below it appears to be nothing more than a big crack in the cliff. It can't be seen from most of the shelf, because it is behind a ledge. From mountaintop to ledge is a sheer drop, and from the ledge down to the shelf is another. The bottom line is I have recently made two more visits to the cave, rappelling down to the upper entrance. Something other-worldly happened to me. I want to go there with you, if you're willing.

I probably should not discuss any of this by email.

Alys

From: jarrett@erikssonphoto.com
To: engberg@stockholmonline.net
Date: Sat Jun 30 4:55 PM EDT
Subj: Re: Alice's Cave

Alys, nothing about Alice's Cave surprises me. I am ready to believe anything. Since you'll be in DC, I can make my point clearly if you'll let me show you a cave artifact I keep in my living room. I doubt you'll spend any more time concerned about your sanity. I live in Baltimore. It's a short train ride from DC, and I'll pick you up. Wednesday is perfect—it's a US holiday.

Yes, I will go to Alice's Cave with you.

I'll see you Wednesday. Call me when you have a moment, and we'll set it up. Or email. Or Skype.

Jarrett

TRIP JOURNAL, Sunday July 1 9:12 PM - I have to say more about Alice's Cave, or this journal won't make sense. I'm dictating this to my phone as I drive. I'll insert it in the journal tomorrow.

Today was awful. I didn't get to sleep until after two this morning. My dreams were all about Alice's Cave, and then I worked a long day, always thinking about yesterday's emails.

I once owned Alice's Cave. I inherited it, along with a ton of land around it, from relatives I didn't know existed. They had received the land as a wedding present in the thirties. They found the cave long ago but kept it secret to protect what it contained—artifacts of a colony of people who lived there for generations, about five thousand years ago. My benefactors left it to me because they admired my cave photography and thought I would be a knowing and responsible owner.

I visited the cave for a few days soon after I learned of the inheritance, with Mira, who wrote the first set of emails, and her husband, Roger. Mira is a professor of anthropology, Roger my friend for decades. The three of us have done a lot of caving. That first trip to Alice's Cave was in the spring. We stayed only three days, but the cave so impressed us that we rearranged our lives and spent the entire summer working there.

The prehistoric people who lived in Alice's Cave were quite advanced. They made cast copper weapons and tools, grew grain, and made rope from their own hemp. The cave was their year-round home, but in summer they lived outdoors on an isolated remote shelf of land high on the wall of a river valley. They left a staggering trove of paintings on the cave walls and on clay tablets. Mira says the cave is an important source of data on late Neolithic culture on the Scandinavian peninsula.

None of this explains the cave's grip on me.

Alice's Cave has a power—a spirit presence. It is strongest in the cave's most beautiful room, with a stream and pool and fine decorations. You sense the spirit the moment you enter the room, and it messes with your dreams forever after. Through the spirit I encountered Alice, for whom we named the cave. She was a girl of about eleven, a real person who lived in the cave long ago. She and I saw each other, and she understood that I would come to the cave in the future. She painted a picture of me on a clay tablet and showed me where she would leave it for me, in a rock crevice. I found nearly a hundred tablets, including the picture of me. Mira dated the paint to five thousand years ago, and it shows my face. I have the tablet under glass in my living room. The rest of the tablets, and the hundreds of feet of richly detailed wall paintings, remain in the cave, except for one tablet Mira kept.

I have seen other caves with spirit presence, but they didn't transport me through time, or whatever the spirit of Alice's Cave did. Even Lechuguilla has never troubled my dreams. Roger and Mira and I did cave diving in Mexico, in sacred Cenotes with artifacts of the

Mayas, and they were spooky indeed. But they didn't change my life. I've never encountered anything like Alice's Cave.

I collaborated with a journalist I had worked with in the past to write a book about the cave, with hundreds of photographs. The book's success lets me take my pick of work now. As always, I choose to go caving. I take cameras and get paid for it, but the important thing is to get underground. That's why I'm driving five hours home after working a long day on not enough sleep.

The cave is now the property of the government of Sweden. I sold my inheritance for one dollar after the book's success removed money as an issue, in exchange for a promise that the cave would be protected and not developed. Under the influence of an activist Minister of Culture, a caver, the government reopened the entrance, which had been closed by a landslide, and installed a gate. The cave became a designated Swedish cultural treasure. I was invited to lead a tour at the dedication, and I met the activist minister herself, Alys Engberg. The same Alys I'll meet with next Wednesday.

Enough. I'm nearly home. I'm too tired to call Mira tonight. That will have to wait. But could someone please explain to me how all this happened on the same day?

I SLEEP LATE and pay for it with a vivid and nerve-wracking dream, the third cave dream in three nights.

> *The spirit chamber! I have been here so often that it seems like home, but I am always aware that the spirit could crush me like a bug. I woke up here two hours ago and have been waiting for something to happen. The cave is chilly—below sixty—and I am not dressed for it. I'm concerned that I might not be able to get out. Where is Alys? She told me she would meet me here.*

Is the cave moving back into the foreground of my life? After our summer expedition, I had cave dreams every night until the book was published. They are less frequent now, but I will probably have dreams of Alice's Cave forever.

I finish my coffee and have begun unpacking when Mira calls on Skype. Roger is with her.

"Did you get home OK? Can you talk now?" Mira sounds tense.

"Sure. I was in bed before midnight and slept most of twelve hours. I dreamed of the spirit chamber. How are you guys doing?"

"I'm having another attack of cave insanity. I've been working for weeks on the program I told you about. It's finally running, and I'm drowning in new information."

Mira and Roger came to dinner three months ago, and I heard a great deal about her idea for postprocessing images of paintings. Some tablets are partially obscured by crazing. Mira's program clears that up somehow. She explained it in her usual way—in rapid-fire Polish English, becoming less and less comprehensible as she got excited.

"At the micro level, the crazing follows jagged patterns that are almost regular—like lightning. Very different from painted lines. When I remove the crazing, it leaves fine detail I've never seen before. Such as me in the upper entrance, on the tablet I used for testing."

"Can you send me that image?"

"Sure." She turns away from Skype briefly. When her email arrives, I have to agree with her—without question, the ancient image shows Mira in modern caving gear.

Mira comes back to Skype. "Each image takes a great deal of my time. I hope to improve the program, but right now the process is slow—days for each one. Even so, I have many new images, and that's not all. Do you remember the time I found myself actually in the scene? I'm sure you haven't forgotten how I flipped out."

"The battle."

"Yesterday, while I was staring at a tablet painting, I slipped into it. Only briefly, but I knew immediately what was happening. I was in the spirit chamber, upstream from the pool. People were holding a ceremony. They had a fire. I could hear them singing. I freaked."

"You don't *sound* freaked."

"You haven't been here," Roger says quietly. "It's déjà vu all over again."

"Now what, Mira? Will you press on?"

"I don't know. To start with, I'm talking to you."

"You don't know the whole story. I've been exchanging email with Alys Engberg, the Culture Minister you met."

"Oh. Her."

I recall that Mira said Alys drove her nuts with questions during the project to reopen the entrance.

"She wants to talk about the cave too. She'll be in DC next week, and we're going to meet."

"Jarrett, I have to get back into the cave. There are things about it we haven't figured out, but that's only the anthropology part of the reason. The cave is pulling on me."

"Me too. I'll call you after I hear from Alys. Maybe we should go together."

Roger's head is in his hands. "Are we ready for this?"

AFTER THE CALL, I finish unpacking my gear and spend the rest of a long day working on the pictures from the shoot. I'll finish them tomorrow.

In the evening I exchange more email with Alys Engberg.

> **From: engberg@stockholmonline.net**
> **To: jarrett@erikssonphoto.com**
> **Date: Mon Jul 2 8:22 PM EDT**
> **Subj: Alice's Cave**
>
> I'm in DC, exhausted. I'll be through tomorrow at four. Are you available for dinner?

> **From: jarrett@erikssonphoto.com**
> **To: engberg@stockholmonline.net**
> **Date: Mon Jul 2 8:29 PM EDT**
> **Subj: Re: Alice's Cave**
>
> Alys - The 5:17 train from DC arrives in Baltimore at six. I'll pick you up. I'm eager to hear about your cave experiences.
>
> See you tomorrow!

I HAVEN'T SEEN ALYS ENGBERG since we met five years ago in Alice's Cave. She wore a caving helmet that day, but in the train station I recognize her immediately. She is an unusual admixture of ethnic types—her face is Nordic in shape but not coloring, with dark hair and eyes. I spent six months preparing the photographs for the book, including many of Alice's self-portraits, and when I met Alys in the cave she seemed like Alice in modern dress.

We go to a fine restaurant in Baltimore, a place I bring prospective clients. We eat well, with a spectacular city view from the table. Alys says she'd rather not discuss her cave experiences in public, so over dinner we talk about other things, including cave photography and the craziness of DC. She's bright and a good conversationalist.

The drive home takes only a few minutes, and on the way I open the discussion of the cave. "Let's begin with my story. I'll confess in advance that the ancient cave artifact in my living room explains everything."

She raises her eyebrows.

I TURN ON THE DISPLAY LIGHTING as we walk into the apartment. "Welcome to Alice's Cave. While you look around and gasp, can I get you a glass of wine?"

I have practiced this theatrical gesture on many visitors.

The walls of my living room are all but papered in photographs from the book, more than a hundred large glossies, extending into the dining room. I spent weeks on the lighting, which is perfect, if I may say so. The ambient light is low; only the photos are fully lit. Bench seats face the wall to make it easier to view the lower photos.

Many of the pictures are of Alice's paintings, showing the people she lived with and the cave as it looked then. Self-portraits show her at various ages. The display also includes my photos of the cave as it is today—the shelf outside, the entrance, the living chamber. And the spirit chamber. Its reflecting pool and glistening columns look the same in Alice's paintings and my photographs, but neither conveys the impact of the place. Only dreams do that. The feeling is too intense to be simply remembered.

My gallery conveys the idea of the cave in a way that always moves me. I can see it moves Alys too. She walks slowly around the room. "This is overwhelming. I miss the sound of the stream. Otherwise I feel I'm there." She is exactly right. I've often thought I should have recorded the sound of the stream. It's a big part of the cave experience, and in my apartment I always notice its absence.

I circle the room with her, lost once again in the images of the cave. When we complete the tour, I bring up the light in the glass display case in the center of the room, with its two paintings of me on an ancient clay tablet.

A moment passes before Alys understands. "Oh! My God. This is *you*." Next to the tablet is Mira's certificate saying the paint was carbon dated to five thousand years.

Alys sinks onto a bench seat and stares up at the tablet.

"This is Alice, the artist. I met her when she was about eleven." I bring up the light on the best of Alice's adult self-portraits, near the display case. She is perhaps twenty, reflected in the spirit chamber's pool. A torch lights her face, and Alys surely sees how much it resembles her own.

Long pause, with an incredulous look.

"You met her?"

"We saw each other."

"So it's not just me. Please tell me the story of these paintings of you."

MY MARRIAGE ENDED not long before Alice's Cave entered my life, and since then I've been free of the distractions women provide. My apartment is a showcase for my pictures of the cave, a museum of which I am director and curator. It is not designed to bring women into my life. But Alys reacts to the cave exactly as I do, and our shared sense of awe leaves me uncomfortable. What is it I fear? A cliff, at the bottom of which lie the jagged rocks of relationship? Acknowledging the essential loneliness of my life?

"Jarrett," Jeannie said as she left, "you need to live alone with your cameras and pictures and your caving. I'm through standing between you and your destiny." Single is both good and bad. Nights alone are balanced by spur-of-the-moment caving trips without explanation or defense. I have often thought of Alys Engberg. From our first meeting I've had the illogical feeling that we've known each other for years. Thousands of years. But Jeannie was right, and in any event I am too busy to make room for a woman in my life.

As I relate the story of the eleven-year-old artist who painted my picture and kept it safe for all that time, I suspect Alys also senses a potential entanglement between us. Does she share my apprehension?

"THE ROUTE FROM THE UPPER ENTRANCE to the spirit chamber is difficult," Alys says. "I am astonished that it was possible without modern equipment. It includes a deep pit—too deep for my seventy meters of rope. I rappelled down to a ledge, saw no way to continue, and gave up."

"You were alone?"

"Yes. I don't like solo caving, but taking another caver would amount to conspiracy to trespass. The current minister has closed the cave to all—to preserve the cave, he says. He is deaf to the argument that much remains to be learned there."

"He must think the cave is secure because the main entrance is gated. He doesn't know about the upper entrance."

"Exactly. I made a second trip two weeks ago and did find my way down to the spirit chamber. It looked exactly as it did when I first saw it. I was overcome with exhaustion. I slept and dreamed—a long, coherent sequence in which I woke up, put on my pack and helmet, and crawled down the passage into the living chamber. I was shocked—it was completely changed. Daylight came directly through the entrance. Only two hearths instead of four. The north wall was unpainted. And the wooden structures looked new, not decayed to dust the way they are now."

"That's how it was in Alice's time. I've seen it that way too."

She looks surprised. "I'd like to hear about that."

"Your dream first. Sorry I interrupted."

"I went out through the entrance, which had no gate. The entrance chamber opened directly onto the shelf. Instead of a mountain of rock, there was a garden of trees and flowering shrubs. I heard children playing and found a carved wooden doll, a toy. I felt I had to carry it into the cave. When I returned to the living chamber, I put the doll into a cargo pocket, took off my pack and helmet, and lay down. That's where the dream ended. I woke in the living chamber as it is today." She pauses for a sip of wine.

"This dream is what made you doubt your sanity?"

"I went to sleep in the spirit chamber and woke up in the living chamber. How did I get there? And the doll! When I woke, it was still in my pocket, not decayed by time. It looked freshly painted."

I refill her wine glass, and we sit in the living room, surrounded by Alice's Cave. "What happened?" she asks quietly. "Did I actually walk through the cave as it was long ago?"

"Alys, you need to read my journal. Something similar happened to me, an impossible dream walk. What did you do with the doll?"

"It's in my safe at home. I couldn't leave it in the cave; it would be an anachronism. The other wooden relics are all but gone. We could date the doll's paint, but we already know the answer."

"Here's another development. My partners in the original exploration were Mira, the archaeologist you met, and Roger, her husband. Mira and I talked a few days ago. She has been analyzing my photographs of Alice's painted tablets, doing digital processing to enhance the images. She has uncovered a painting of herself at the upper entrance."

"Another strange occurrence."

"More than you know. Mira never went to the upper entrance. She's a scientist, and impossibilities don't sit well with her."

"I remember her clearly. She spent most of that summer on the shelf on behalf of potential artifacts the construction could damage. She is—a very strong woman."

I remember Mira's description of Alys, who rubbed Mira the wrong way. To be honest, that's not difficult. Mira is Polish—brilliant, excitable, with a mighty wrath but quick to forgive. Including her and Alys on the same trip could be a mistake.

"Roger is a geologist. He and I were caving buddies in high school. Mira and Roger have been caving with me for many years, which is why I took them with me to explore Alice's Cave. Now Mira wants to go back."

"I do too. I feel I must. We could go together, I suppose. But you should tell Mira and Roger that the trip would have to be covert. For you and them, the consequences of being found out would not be severe. You might be barred from entering Sweden; you wouldn't go to prison. I probably would, as a former government official. But I made two trips anyway, and I want to go again despite the risk of public shame if we should be caught."

We sit at length, sipping our wine. It is after eleven. Finally we both speak at the same time. She breaks off, and I continue. "Alys, I have a second bedroom. It's fully stocked with everything you might need. My clients sometimes use it. You're welcome to stay if you'd like, or I can take you back to the train station, as unappealing as that must sound at this time of night."

She laughs. "I had started to say it's late, and I had best start back. But I'd be much happier in your second bedroom. Thank you."

"When do you have to reappear in DC? Mira and Roger live nearby. Would you be interested in discussing a trip with them?"

"I would be interested in anything that will get us into Alice's Cave quickly. Tomorrow and Friday I'm free. I have meetings all day Thursday in DC, and on Saturday I leave."

"You're welcome to spend tomorrow night here too."

ANOTHER CAVE DREAM, the fourth in five nights.

> *I am sitting at the top of the breakdown in the spirit chamber. Alys had planned to join me here, and I am anxious because she has not appeared. Has she encountered some mishap? Solo caving is risky. Now I see she is already here, sitting in Alice's spot on the flowstone in the pool. How did I miss her? When I make my way down to her, I see that she is not Alys, but Alice, now a beautiful*

young woman of perhaps twenty-five. She smiles and says, "I've been waiting for you." I look again and see that she is Alys, and that we are in my living room.

Alys's visit and the impending meeting with Mira and Roger—we exchanged email last night, and they will be here for dinner—are only the most recent symptoms that the cave is coming back into my life. Impossibilities lie everywhere, like Mira's paintings and Alys's doll, not to mention that everything is happening at once. It started less than four days ago but has already built up speed that makes me wary about losing control over my life.

ALYS AND I WALK to my favorite little diner for breakfast, and as we eat I tell her of my dream and hear about hers. She too has cave dreams regularly now, part of the reason she had feared for her stability. Her dream last night was like mine, of both of us in the cave, yet another sign of linkage between us. Why does that make me nervous? Perhaps because it seems I have no choice in the matter. She's beautiful, young—not yet forty—friendly, thoughtful, and a polished success. Also passionate about the cave. But I feel like a train is coming and I'm tied to the track.

"My obsession with the cave," she says, "has ended my political ambitions. The cave makes them seem shallow. I feel that it came into my life to teach me there's more in my future than a post in government. My father was a diplomat. He raised me by himself after my mother died when I was twelve. He never married again, but focused his life on grooming me for a government career. His greatest accomplishment was my appointment as Minister of Culture. He died shortly after that, convinced that I was on my way to being the first female prime minister. The cave interrupted that life plan. I first saw it in your book. I wanted to meet you then. Seeing the paintings and the spirit chamber in person was the final straw for my political self. I realized I needed to do something more important with my life than attend meetings and shuffle papers."

"Where did you get your native-speaker English? You sound like you were raised here."

"I was, part of the time. My mother was American, and I grew up back and forth between Stockholm and DC. I'm a Swedish citizen because my father was Swedish and a US citizen by birth. I learned about caves in the high school caving club, in Virginia. I've been in a lot of caves, but never anything like Alice's."

"You're a DC girl! It makes me laugh that I explained how the Fourth is a US Holiday. Sorry. What is it you're doing in DC this week?"

"Visiting you. Earning my living, consulting for an NGO, working on a fishing rights issue that seems trivial compared to the cave. I scheduled the trip for this week because I love being in the US on the Fourth. It reminds me of fireworks shows when I was a kid."

FOR MUCH OF THE DAY, Alys immerses herself in my 300-page journal of the summer in the cave. It should dispel her fear that she's unstable, because it describes my dreams, including walking through the ancient cave to the spirit chamber and then waking up there. The journal also tells of Mira studying a painting of a battle and slipping into the scene. And of my meeting Alice. This evening we'll grill steaks on the balcony and talk about the possibility of a joint expedition. But we will surely also discuss what's in the journal.

Alys rubs her eyes. "It's good of you to let me read this. I assume Roger and Mira have seen it, and no one else."

"Right."

"Your dream, where you woke up in the spirit chamber, is like what happened to me. Didn't you worry about your sanity?"

"Not as much as Mira worried when she found herself in the ancient time."

"Now that I see I'm not alone, I'm hungry for more. I feel I'll learn something vital about myself in the cave."

I pour wine and put out bread and cheese. We sit quietly eating and drinking, and as Alys finishes the journal I read it over her shoulder. Eventually she walks over to the display case, looks long at Alice's painting of my face, and then turns to a self-portrait of the adult Alice and stands looking at it.

"How odd, that she and I have the same name."

"They don't seem the same to me."

"How did you learn her name, Jarrett?"

"Heard it in a dream."

"Naturally, the English spelling is what occurred to you. It's a very old name in many cultures. The spelling is unimportant."

"The name does fit you. When we first met, you looked so much like Alice that I flashed on the idea of you being her."

She refills our glasses, and it occurs to me that she is struggling with how much to say.

She walks to a photograph of the spirit chamber and turns to me. "When we met, I already knew you from a dream I had during the construction project. I was blown away by the paintings and the living chamber, and when Mira took me to the spirit chamber I felt I had come home. Our camp was outside on the shelf. I woke up in the middle of the night and went to the spirit chamber alone. I slept there and dreamed about you. I was a young girl, seeing you as Alice did. And yes, I have pictures of myself at twelve that look just like her."

She returns to the dining table, where she looks at her hands and then up at me. Her resemblance to Alice is uncanny.

OPENING UP TO ALYS is easy now. "The cave changed the way I see the world. It showed me a spirit reality that exists alongside the laws of physics. I've always felt the power of special places, but without conceding the reality of spirit. My dream walk between our time and Alice's time was physically impossible. Yours too. You brought back a brand-new ancient toy. I gave Alice a key ring in a dream, and later, on the one occasion when we met in my waking life, I saw the key ring on a cord around her neck."

"By that point in your journal, I was skimming. I didn't realize you and Alice met except in dreams."

"Alys, I tell you, she walked out of the cave, right up to our tents out on the shelf, and took my hand. She led me to the spirit chamber to see the funeral ceremony for her grandfather. I was wide awake. I had no choice but to surrender my skepticism."

We sip wine. Alys looks like a woman vindicated, but she's shocked too.

Eventually I continue. "Once I believed, my dream communication with Alice became more intense. She led me to her hiding place where she intended to put the painting of me. She put tablets there throughout her life. After I found them, I dreamed of showing her a tablet she hadn't painted yet—this one." I bring up the light on the photo. "That's Alice with her husband and her first baby. She understood immediately that it was a tablet she would paint later, a revelation of her future. I saw it in her eyes."

Alys looks at the photo. "The revelation I crave is of my past, not the future. I have hints of an ancient time in dreams and in accidental glimpses into my subconscious."

"I was married for ten years to a woman who attended lectures by every spiritual guru who came to town. She read dozens of books on the subject. I thought it was all fraud. It's ironic that I met the spirit chamber after she and I split up."

"You surprise me, Jarrett. Your books and this apartment show sensitivity of spirit. Your book on Alice's Cave comes alarmingly close to giving the feeling of the spirit chamber. I would not have picked you for someone who denied spirit influence."

"That was the past. Before the spirit chamber."

"The cave changed me, too. As a government minister, I had to interact with people in an artificial way and do what was needed, whatever my own feelings. My experiences in the cave went too deep for me to put aside. The cave demands my full attention. That's why I left the government. That's why I'm here."

"We're pretty funny, the cold-eyed government official and the cave photographer with his head full of images and f-stops. What a team to seek what the spirit has to give us."

"Well, Mr. Photographer, this cold-eyed government official would like another glass of wine, please."

ALYS AND I ARE INTO THE SECOND BOTTLE of wine when Roger and Mira arrive. We have plowed our way through enough bread and cheese to stock a deli, so we remain reasonably sober, but we are laughing together when I open the door.

Roger and Mira exchange a look. "We seem to have missed some of the party," Mira says.

"Mira, you have no idea. We've covered a lot of ground. Let me introduce Alys Engberg, covert explorer of Alice's Cave. Alys, my friends and colleagues Mira and Roger Kramnick."

I am relieved to see Mira smile. "Alys and I met when the cave was reopened. Alys, I'm afraid I was short with you. Please forgive me."

"You were working eighteen-hour days and still found time to teach me about the cave. I'm grateful. It's good to see you, Mira. And to meet you, Roger."

My worries about Alys and Mira abate. Somewhat.

I hand Roger and Mira glasses of wine. "We've been trading stories. Alys has some impossible experiences, not so different from ours. If I hadn't plied her with wine I'd probably not have heard about them. We can talk over dinner, but the bottom line is a cave trip. Soon."

"I went in through the upper entrance two weeks ago," Alys says. "I slept in the spirit chamber and dreamed my way into the living chamber, which had only two hearths, and the entry chamber wasn't closed by breakdown. Out on the shelf, I picked up a wooden toy and brought it back into the cave. I woke in the living chamber as it is today, but I still had the toy, in like-new condition. That's why I'm here. I thought the cave was making me crazy."

"That's why we drank two bottles of wine," I say.

Mira and Roger exchange another look.

AFTER DINNER, the four of us sit around an enlarged photograph of the big cave map while Alys shows us her route from the upper entrance to the spirit chamber. "This is a hundred-meter pit," she says, with her finger on the map. "How on earth did they manage it without modern rigging? It looks flat-out impossible."

"They might have used another route," Roger says. "Perhaps one that no longer exists. Have you been to the west entrance? It's closed now, but it was obviously used at some point."

Alys shakes her head. "My entire acquaintance with the cave consists of the living chamber, the spirit chamber, and this route."

Roger nods. "We think Alice's mother drew the map, because she is standing beside it in one of Alice's paintings. The upper entrance is at the very top of the map—actually off the top, like an afterthought. Perhaps the map was already complete when the upper entrance was discovered. There could be a way there that simply wouldn't fit on the wall."

"I did see leads going westward." Alys is mapping the possibilities in her mind.

"Jarrett and I saw some tantalizing leads near the old entrance, but we didn't have time to pursue them. The original people were accomplished cavers and climbers. They descended from the shelf to the river and climbed back. They negotiated pits in the cave. They had good rope, since they grew hemp."

"They used hide rope at first," Mira says. "The paintings show them plaiting it."

We sit staring at the cave map and sipping wine.

"Time for show and tell." Mira reaches into her computer case. "I want you to see what has me so stirred up. Jarrett, can you find your picture of tablet eighty-three?"

That picture is not on my wall. I find the print in the file cabinet and lay it on top of the cave map. The image isn't clear; crazing in the paint interferes with details. The tablet has three panels. The lower half shows a cave entrance, from the inside. The interior of the cave is a muddle of crazing.

"The upper entrance!" Alys says, as happily as if she'd seen a picture of a friend.

"Yes," Mira says. "Has Jarrett told you what I've been doing?"

"He said you were enhancing images and found a picture of yourself at the upper entrance, where you've never been."

Mira points to the photo. "See how the crazing obscures the image? It hides many fine painted lines. I wrote a program that finds and deletes the crazing, which is characteristically jagged. Here's the output, showing the painted lines without the crazing."

She puts her laptop on the table and brings up a revised version of the photo. Inside the entrance, the impenetrable thicket of paint crazing is replaced by a sketch of a woman wearing a caving suit. She is sitting beside her pack. Her helmet and several coils of rope lie beside her. Her face is clear. She is unquestionably Mira.

ALYS IS TAKEN ABACK. She stares at my photo of the tablet and then at Mira's reconstruction.

"I wouldn't have believed this if I hadn't seen Jarrett's face on the tablet in the display case. Alice *must* have seen you, Mira."

"I certainly never saw her. I've thought of nothing else but this image for days. I swear I've never been to the upper entrance, but obviously I will go there, so she can see me and paint this tablet. My future, revealed in the past." Mira drops her head into her hands. "This scrambles my brain."

"How sure are we that Alice actually saw Mira?" Roger is always the scientist. "The sketch could be no more than an artifact of Mira's program. Strange things happen in image processing."

Mira reacts like a wounded bear. "Roger Kramnick! You know better. I've shown you a dozen versions of the output, made with different algorithms. They're all different, but every one of them happens to look exactly like me."

Another long silence, and then she goes on. "I think it's scary. I'm almost afraid to go, but I must. Since I saw the sketch, the cave has been pulling me in. Now you appear, Alys, looking totally like an adult Alice in good clothes, and the resemblance is no accident. The spirit chamber has hooked us all!"

Roger looks at her and then at me and Alys. "I can see it coming, and I can't do a thing about it." He sounds resigned. "The cave is one of a kind. We've seen other spooky caves, but they don't disturb our dreams. We all got a bit crazy that summer. If we go back it will happen again. I'm not looking forward to that."

"You're not listening," Mira snaps. "It's *already* happening again. Of course," she adds sweetly, "you could stay home."

"I don't think so. The cave is pulling on me, too."

IT IS PAST ELEVEN before we pack up. We have hammered out a detailed plan for a ten-day expedition to Alice's Cave. Roger and Mira and I will fly a week from Friday. I make printed copies for everyone.

Clearing our schedules will be surprisingly easy. Mira is off for the summer. Roger will take vacation from his government job. I have nothing scheduled until August, and Alys will simply declare herself unavailable for that time.

We will have a week in the cave. Alys's SUV will carry us. We will establish a base camp in the trees near the top of the mountain and make repeated trips through the upper entrance. We'll buy our supplies in Stockholm. The bulk of the stores can stay in the SUV, and we'll make mostly day trips into the cave, except that we will sometimes sleep in the spirit chamber.

Alys shakes hands with Roger and Mira as they leave. "I hope Jarrett told you this trip must be secret."

"He mentioned it," Mira says, "but I don't care. I have to go. If we weren't going as a group I would still go—alone, if necessary."

"I hate having this illegal expedition on paper," Alys says. "Please treat the plan as confidential. I am committing a high crime against the people of Sweden by planning to enter the cave."

We are all excited. Even Roger.

I DRIVE ALYS TO THE TRAIN STATION in the morning. She has a ten o'clock meeting in DC, with a stop at her hotel first. She'll be there by eight, with time for a one-hour power nap. We find ourselves in the breakfast bar at the train station at 6:15, twenty minutes before her train.

She looks at me. "We're starting down a foggy path. We have no idea where it leads."

"We barely had time to plan the necessities last night. We didn't get to what we might find."

"Think about it. I'll call you on Skype when I get home. You and I particularly need to discuss it."

"What do you mean?" We walk toward the platform.

"Jarrett, the cave is pulling us together. Interlocking dreams. Mutual recognition when we first met. Our shared enjoyment of our time together this week. That makes it important for you to know I don't want us to get involved."

Her words do not ease my feeling of being tied to the track, not even a little bit. Yes, the cave is pulling us together, and in the most insidious way—by playing on my touching contact with a little girl who lived in three thousand BC. Now Alys has raised the topic. She's thinking about it too.

She puts down her bags and hugs me. "Thank you for treating me so kindly. I asked you to go with me to the spirit chamber because you know the cave best of anyone, and the cave has something to teach me. I'm looking forward to this adventure."

She steps aboard the train and waves as it departs. How fitting, I think, that she arrived and left on a train.

I THINK ABOUT THE RUSH OF TIME as I lie awake in the early morning.

I need this time for myself and rejoice that the children are still asleep, a gift of the thrum of summer rain on the thatch, masking the waking sounds of our small village. The dog is alert, straining to hear the dangers she is sure threaten me and the children. She is anxious because Kyle is away; he left ten days ago on a trading trip to Rivermouth with Father and Brandr. She pads to my bed and noses my hand, and before lying down again she checks all three children. Her work is never done.

Fourteen years have passed since the summer I dreamed of a painting—my own painting—of Kyle and me with our baby. I was eleven then, still a little girl. I painted that picture years later, long after Yrsa was born. Did the spirit change my life by showing me the image? Or simply reveal my future?

In the dream, a man showed me the painting. His name was Jered, and I will never forget him. I dreamed of him several times that summer. He will not visit the spirit chamber as a living man for many years, but even at eleven I understood that time means nothing to the spirit. I thought I would never see Jered again, but Aunt Inge said I would, and now I'm sure she was right.

I was too young then to fear the day when all our elders would be gone. Grandfather Zoan died that summer—the first loss—but even then I didn't foresee the loneliness I feel without them. I was happy to have their advice and never imagined this time of fear and danger, when I need them more than ever, particularly Grandmother Quitana and Aunt Inge. In the spirit chamber, I dream of them and speak to them and weep with the joy of it. Mother has always told me—this from Aunt Inge, she says—to make waking decisions about my life and not to rely entirely on dreams. But my dream visits with the lost elders are happy ones, and the spirit would never lead me astray.

WHEN KYLE AND UNCLE ARAMEL began building houses near the river, I was torn by conflict. I knew by then that Kyle and I would marry, but I couldn't bear the idea of living where visiting the spirit chamber would be impossible during winter storms. We commonly see ten-day periods of bad weather, and I have never in my life had even three days without time in the spirit chamber.

Then Aunt Angela's boys—my cousins Bjorn and Soren—found a way to the Riverside Cave from the main cave. We had known the Riverside Cave for years. Uncle Aramel and Uncle Druian found it when they were boys; Mother says they often hid in it. It's a tunnel, a gentle climb that leads far into the mountain to a room with a domed ceiling so high that it can barely be seen in torchlight. Bjorn risked his life to climb to that ceiling. He has some of Grandfather in him; Grandfather's climbing exploits are legend.

At the top of the climb Bjorn followed an easy passage to a hidden entry into a gigantic room that he recognized as the cavern west of the spirit chamber. In all the years we passed through that room on the way to the west entrance, we never guessed that it concealed an easy route to the river. Bjorn hung a rope there, and it makes the climb easy enough that we can all do it. The day he hung that rope, Aunt Inge laughed as she climbed it, and she was fifty. I thought she would live forever.

WE CALL THIS PLACE THE RIVERSIDE, with its four houses. I am happy here, for I love having my own house.

I use the Riverside Cave every other day to reach the spirit chamber, while my cousin Astrid watches her children and mine. We take turns at that task. She and Soren live next to us, with their own three children. Uncle Aramel and Brandr live in the third house with Ingrid, Brandr's young wife from Rivermouth. The fourth house, the newest one, is for Kyle's brother Leif, his wife Dota, and their five children.

When Ingrid's baby is born the Riverside will have twenty-two people. More than sixty live on the bench and in the cave, and as our community grows, more and more will move to the Riverside. The men have already cut the posts for a fifth house.

JERED CAME BACK into my dreams the night of the midsummer festival, after Mother told of Uncle Sigurd warning us to beware attack by enemies. Since that night I have dreamed of Jered regularly. Sometimes in the dreams I am eleven, sometimes an adult.

Jered will come here again, and I will see him, through the spirit. It is no coincidence that I dreamed of him the same night Mother gave us Uncle Sigurd's warning. The spirit is at work in all these dreams, and Jered's coming is connected to the danger Uncle Sigurd was concerned about.

I am afraid, for my children's lives depend on me. I must be patient, though, and wait to learn what Jered's visit will bring. I can think of nothing else.

EXHAUSTION SETS IN as I drive home from the train station. I'm not a kid anymore; fifty is behind me. I feel as if I've been running full tilt for the five days since the email exchanges of last Saturday. I got home late Sunday night after working two days in a cold dark cave in New Hampshire. OK, I admit that most caves are cold and dark, but those were long days and the nights were short. By the time I got home I was toast. Monday and Tuesday I worked on the shots from that job. I sent off the results an hour before I picked up Alys at the train station. Since then I have been entertaining a guest—a remarkable woman, but a houseguest nonetheless.

Now I'm off duty, at least until Alys calls me from Stockholm. The situation calls for a nap. Twenty minutes after I reach home I'm in bed.

We pick our way across a vast rubble field. Alys is hurting from her fall, and the uneven footing slows her down. She tries not to show her pain. "Let's rest," I say. "You need it."

We sit on a low, flat boulder, shuck off our packs, and lie back, tired. I wake in the dark, look toward Alys, and find her asleep near me. I can see no sky at all; we are in a cavern. Dim light comes from a small flowing stream. This place is familiar. I should recognize it.

Alys stirs, and I ask her where we are. She speaks, but I don't understand the language. We are in the spirit chamber! We struggle out to the living chamber, and for the first time I see its original state—beautiful, enormous, and utterly empty. We walk through it and out onto the shelf. Bees work midsummer flowers, and birds are everywhere.

Looking toward the mountaintop, I recognize the upper entrance in the cliff face. I expect something to happen. Two people appear. One by one, they descend a rope and disappear into the upper entrance. They are unaware of the danger awaiting them. I try to shout to warn them, but no sound comes.

I look at Alys; she has been watching and knows the hazard. We both recognize that the danger is to us, that this dream is a message.

THE DREAM SEQUENCE seems to last for hours. I wake at noon in a feverish sweat, writhing with anxiety because I must warn the two explorers of their peril. My mind doesn't clear until I've showered and had coffee.

I think about the dream as I work. So many images! The difficult rubble field, and Alys injured. A time before Alice's people came to the cave. That part doesn't startle me. Caves change slowly; Alice's Cave waited empty for long ages before people found it, and it has changed little to this day.

The dream showed us as a couple in an ancient time, but what can I make of Alys speaking in a strange language? And what of the danger of the upper entrance? A clear warning from the spirit chamber. Should I tell the others?

I'M STILL PONDERING when the phone rings. I glance at the clock: 2:45 PM.

"Jarrett? It's Alys. Hi."

"Alys! I had an incredible dream this morning. I need to tell you about it. Do you have time to talk?"

"Is your spare bedroom still available?"

"For you? Of course. What changed?"

"My morning meeting was moved forward to nine and was done by 11:30. The afternoon was canceled. So I napped in my room from noon until half an hour ago. I had a frightening dream about the cave."

"We should exchange dreams."

"I've also had some unsettling news from home, and I've canceled my flight. I can think of nothing but the cave. I need to talk to you. Shall I simply take a cab?"

"Hell, no. Call me from DC when you know what train you'll be on. I'll pick you up."

I'm glad I already had my nap. Should I call Mira and Roger? I decide to wait until I hear what Alys has to say.

AT THE TRAIN STATION, Alys looks her usual composed self. She travels light, with a laptop bag and a single suitcase. I load them into the trunk and help her into the car.

"I'm awfully glad to see you," she says, and her voice reveals her tension. "You're the only person in my life who would understand the dream. I hope you intend to feed me. I had to run for the train. I haven't eaten since our breakfast in the station."

We stop at my favorite deli, which is deserted this afternoon. Alys is eager to tell her story. "I was relieved to reach you. The dream left me shaking. You and I were in the cave. I was the young Alice. I could see you but not talk to you. I knew I was dreaming, but all my attempts to wake up failed. I would shrug it off, but in the dream I was lying in the spirit chamber. That seems like a stamp of validity."

She falls silent, radiating anxiety. Eventually she relaxes and looks down at her untouched sandwich. "Well. I feel better for telling it, and I *am* starved."

I struggle to absorb her dream. "Caught in the ancient time! On the one hand, it's just a dream."

She finishes without missing a beat. "On the other, a dream lies behind the tablet in your living room."

IN MY APARTMENT, I hand Alys a glass of wine and sit across from her. I glance up to find her looking at me as she did the day we first met in the cave, with the unguarded directness she shares with young Alice. My nervousness about a relationship returns full force. I'm thinking about what to say when she broaches the subject.

"Before we start on dreams, I need to apologize for sounding harsh this morning. I'm sorry. I do want to avoid getting involved, because the energy that would consume is more than I have available when the cave is eating me alive. I know you see that the cave is bringing us together. But every time I have loved a man I have regretted it later. Alice's Cave holds some key to my spirit, and you have a role to play in finding it. I knew that much as soon as I read your book. A relationship would risk all that." She falls silent, although I can see she hasn't finished.

"Alys, this conversation has been too long coming. Yes, the cave is bringing us together, and I feel as you do. My marriage taught me that one should be cautious about relationships, much more than I was. I enjoy life as a single man. But time with you is a pleasure. It will be fun to see the cave together, and I suspect we both have something important to learn."

Alys laughs and relaxes. "We are alike in many ways. We've both been thinking the same thing—not saying it for fear of using the loaded words love and relationship. I'd like to hear about your dream. But I need a hug first, now that we're forewarned."

She is up and in my arms in a flash. The hug does not relieve my concerns, and I know she feels my reticence. Still, the discussion has lowered the tension.

I RELATE THE DREAM by reading my notes, the ones I copied into this journal.

"That's the sort of imagery I was talking about," she says. "Us as a couple. An injury. Another language. And a warning that dovetails with my being trapped in the dream experience."

"You were the young Alice. In my own dreams I am always myself."

She smiles. "I was the young Alice, awed by you, in my first dream, before we met."

"It's a surprise to have you back. I'm glad you're here." We are comfortable together, talking without fencing. The table between us holds walnuts and grapes and cheese. Our bottle of wine is still half full.

The frank look again. "We need to go to the cave by ourselves, Jarrett. We have our own reasons. Mira evidently appeared to Alice at the upper entrance, but she doesn't have hints of being linked to the place or the people. You and I and the cave are connected. By going there together we might discover something about ourselves."

"You mean right away?"

"Yes, but a complication has arisen. My housekeeping service called to tell me my apartment has been burglarized. They say the place is a disaster. I think I know who did it. I developed a stalker while I was at the Ministry. He called me repeatedly until I got unlisted numbers. He harassed me by text, fax, email, and postal mail. He hung out in front of my apartment building and sometimes followed my car. He left notes on my car. I've seen him many times from a distance, always wearing weird black clothes."

"Is he dangerous, or simply crazy?"

"The police think he's not dangerous, but he has been a nuisance for years. One of the things taken in the burglary was my desktop system, which has all my schedules, passwords, and journals. I'm not concerned about my bank accounts, because using them requires an app I run on my phone, and I changed all my passwords right away. My housekeeping service will make the apartment presentable, and my data is all backed up. But my desktop is full of detail about the cave, so it's possible that this jerk, this stalker, could appear there. Also, he knows my car, so I don't think we should use it."

"We don't have to use your car. We can rent one."

"Can't go off-road in a rental. I have a caver friend who will lend us a car. Mine can stay in my apartment garage."

"You're serious? You want to go right away?"

"I had intended to take a Saturday flight to London, stay with a friend Sunday night, and go on to Stockholm Monday. The creep has my flight schedule, so when I don't arrive, he will know it. I'm thinking of skipping London, flying direct to Stockholm, borrowing the car, stopping at my apartment to get my gear, and heading for the cave."

She looks at me again. "What about you? Are you willing to come to Alice's Cave with me, leaving Saturday? There's no better way to see Sweden than with a Swedish girl."

Swedish girl indeed.

"I'll have to push to be ready by Saturday morning," I say, and her face lights up in a smile.

ALYS SETS OUT to make the reservations and arrangements. I call Mira on Skype. "Hi there. Change of plans."

"What?"

"Alys and I are leaving Saturday morning. We both had upsetting spirit chamber dreams, with danger, and we feel we need to go right away."

Long silence.

"I thought Alys had left."

"She did. She napped in DC and was so upset by her dream that she canceled her flight back and returned here this afternoon. We've just decided what to do. You're the first to know."

"Jarrett, we had it all planned. Why can't we stay with that? Roger and I can't leave here before next Friday."

"Because of the dreams from the spirit chamber. I knew you were both committed next week. You should fly as we planned. If Alys and I are back in Stockholm by then, we'll pick you up. If we're in the cave I'll rent you a car, and let you know. You still have that satellite phone account, yes?"

Another silence.

"What kind of danger?"

"Don't know. My dream and hers were different, but both were threatening."

"I should have realized everything would be different. Roger and I laughed at the two of you and wondered how long it would be until you're living on the same side of the Atlantic. It's OK, the change in plans."

"Thanks for your approval."

"I have my own surprise. I finished de-scratching another tablet, and it shows something new—a connection to another cave. In the painting of the houses down near the river, did you remember that behind them is an obvious cave entrance?"

"Yes. We assumed it was a separate cave. It's not on the big map in the living chamber."

"It connects to the big chamber west of the spirit chamber. I'll email you a copy. We should check it out."

"Of course! That explains how they went back and forth between the main cave and the houses on the river. I'll look for the email. And I'll see you next weekend, one way or the other."

"You're leaving Saturday? Do you need supplies, or help?"

"I'll call if I do, but I think I have everything. Thanks."

"Be careful, Jarrett. Don't get hurt."

ALYS DRUMS HER FINGERS as she listens to the airline's wallpaper music. I go to the gear room to start assembling equipment. We'll buy the food in Stockholm, but long trips demand extra consumables; we'll shop tomorrow.

Eventually Alys puts her head into the room. She is clearly astonished. "Oh, my God. So this is what a pro caver's storeroom looks like. I had no idea."

The room was originally a small study. I've put shelves on three walls, with pegs on the fourth, currently holding thousands of feet of coiled rope. One wall is dedicated to photography and computers—cameras, lenses, cases, tripods, flash units, two laptops, several hard drives, solar chargers, batteries, power strips, and a portable flat-screen LCD monitor I use in the field. The other two walls have caving gear—suits and gloves for all conditions, packs, lights, my helmet plus a spare, pry bars and other digging gear, respirators and portable air supplies, harnesses, rappel racks, ascenders, and a ton of miscellaneous rigging. Shipping cases are stacked in one corner. I can outfit three people from this room. I could outfit Alys, but I know she would prefer her own gear.

Alys surveys the room, walks over to the shelf of headlamps, and picks up a brand-new LED unit that cost almost three hundred dollars. She laughs. "You fly first class. This stuff makes my gear look shabby."

"When we first met, your shabby helmet was a badge of experience. That's how I knew you were a caver."

She smiles. "We fly late Saturday morning."

I have stacked the basic gear near the door; together we move it into the living room and make a shopping list. We have a lot of preparation to do tomorrow.

I WAKE FRIDAY MORNING to the smell of frying bacon and find Alys busy in the kitchen. She is talking on her cell phone. "He's right here. Maybe he'll speak to you." She turns to me. "An old caving buddy. Her name is Helen. She's in London. She'd like to tell you what she thinks of your book." She puts her phone on speaker and sets it on the countertop.

"Jarrett Eriksson! Is it really you?" Helen's accent is very Brit. "You can't imagine how good it makes me feel to tell you that *Spirit Chamber* is the most beautiful book I ever saw." At about this point I realize Helen is drinking. "I've tried for years to get Alys to take me there, but she says the cave is closed off now. Congratulations on a wonderful book. Alys says you're going caving but won't tell me where, as usual. Let me tell you," she says in a confidential tone, "if you don't treat her right, you'll have to answer to me. She's been your biggest fan for years. She was excited to meet you in the cave, long ago. She needs a man who appreciates how amazing she is."

Alys rolls her eyes.

Extricating myself from the phone call takes forever. Alys is laughing, and I realize she passed the call to me to escape it herself. "I had planned to spend Sunday night with her. She never drinks when I'm around—only when she's alone. It's hard to talk to her when she's been drinking. I admit to dumping the call on you, but I didn't expect the advice about how to treat me. Sorry."

After breakfast we head out for shopping, and four hours later we return with armloads of stuff. I finish carrying gear from the car and drag out the shipping boxes. Alys lays out the food we bought and opens a bottle of wine.

It is midafternoon, and we're both hungry. We have just settled down to our lunch when the doorbell rings. My puzzlement turns to irritation when I open the door to Joel Harte, the journalist co-author of *Spirit Chamber* and a long-time colleague, friend, and adversary.

"Jarrett! How nice! I didn't expect lunch." As he enters, he sees Alys and does a double take. "I know you, don't I?"

"Alys, this is Joel Harte. Joel, meet Alys Engberg, who was Sweden's Minister of Culture during the reopening of Alice's Cave."

"Joel Harte? The author of *Spirit Chamber*? I'm honored." Alys stands and offers her hand.

Joel smiles. "You're too kind." He takes in the room. "A caving trip?"

"Joel, why are you here?" My irritation is undoubtedly plain in my voice.

"I'd like to tell you it was my sixth sense, but the truth is I saw you downtown."

"What are you even doing in Baltimore?"

"Coming to worship at your shrine, perhaps. Actually, I'm here this week for an association meeting—the SPJ. I planned to call you today anyway to see what you're working on. And surprise! I stumble into yet one more secret expedition in preparation, to our favorite cave!"

OK, I admit it's obvious. Cave gear stacked in the living room, and Alys here.

"Isn't Alice's Cave closed? Are we planning to violate some rules?"

"Joel, as usual, you're wearing out your welcome. What we're doing is none of your business."

"As usual, you make the mistake of thinking that matters to me. All I care about is the story." He bends down to the coffee table and picks up a copy of the trip plan. He glances through it. "Ah. Roger and Mira too. Must be important. Perhaps I'll join you. I'll be in Europe anyway."

"Why don't you two sit down and eat something," Alys says, "before it comes to fisticuffs."

By the time Joel leaves, Alys is annoyed too. "He acted like a jerk."

"He makes a practice of that. I've known him for many years. He has treated me exactly as he did today ever since he and I did the Lechuguilla book. He horned in on our Alice's Cave expedition unasked. Eventually I always forgive him, because our joint projects have come out well."

"He intimated that if we're doing an illegal cave trip, we're vulnerable."

"He wouldn't rat us out, if that's what you mean. He's quite straightforward. He smells a story and wants it. His heart isn't misplaced. Only his manners."

"Will he really come to the cave?"

"I wouldn't be surprised. Appearing uninvited is his specialty."

By day's end we have crammed our gear into three large shipping boxes. Alys looks them over. "It's been an interesting lesson to see how you get ready for a trip. In exchange, let me buy your dinner." This leads to our finishing the day in another restaurant.

"It's fun to spend time with you," she says, as we return to the apartment.

"That's good, because lots more is coming right up, starting tomorrow morning."

Alys reserved a two-room hotel suite in Stockholm for Sunday night and printed boarding passes for tomorrow's flight, which departs at noon. We'll leave here at eight by cab, and it will need to be an SUV.

"Let me pay for this stuff, please," I say.

"Absolutely not. Straight dutch, or no deal. Too involved and involving to have you pay for me."

23

SUMMER ON THE RIVERSIDE is beautiful in a way new to me, for I grew up on the Benchland, with its warm morning sunlight and a beautiful view eastward. The river is only a distant feature of that view, always present but never overwhelming. Here, the river is the heart and soul of our village. It changes with the seasons—roaring in springtime, sparkling and full in summer, tranquil in autumn, quiet in winter, with ice near the banks. Birds flock near the river to fish. Bears fish too, but they prefer the open far side to our steep bank. I see deer, beaver, weasels, foxes, and wolves, plus sometimes a small herd of aurochs, although only rarely now. Father says aurochs were more common where he grew up with Grandmother Folke. Overhead we have hunting birds—hawks by day, owls by night—and many small songbirds. Once a visiting traveler said our birds would make a lovely soup, but I'm not that hungry.

The Riverside is like a smaller version of the Benchland, except that it has access to the river. The entrance to the Riverside Cave is sheltered by a cavern ceiling, like the Benchland's entry cavern but not as high. It protects our animal sheds against winter cold and storms. Our four houses are set beside the cave entrance, near a bank above a steep stretch of the river. The men built the houses back against the rock wall rather than perched on the very bank, where cold winter winds would make our lives miserable. All four houses face southeast, with a view down the river, which curves eastward after it leaves the Benchland. The hills across the river are low enough that early-morning sun warms the house on clear days, except at midwinter. In summer we leave the window unshuttered, and I can see the river rushing toward the sea, throwing veils of spray as it crashes over rocks.

I have seen the sea at Rivermouth, where our river comes to the end of its journey. Standing beside the road watching the water, I heard the song of our spirit chamber. Does that watery trip take a morning, or a day? I would like to know. Things floating in the river move much faster than I can walk. Grandmother Quitana would know, but I can no longer ask her. The men think it's a silly question and don't take it seriously.

Near the houses, the Riverside is narrow. Only a little upstream, the high rock wall behind the houses comes almost to the lip of the steep riverbank, and as we walk the path we must pick our way carefully along the top of the bank. Farther downstream, the Riverside is much wider. Mother and I planted seeds of our Benchland grain in a field there, and this summer we will harvest a huge crop, if our goats don't eat it. Kyle built a wooden fence to keep the goats out, but they sometimes jump over it. We have two dogs to keep the goats from straying. In the afternoon, the dogs herd the goats into their pen so Astrid or I can milk them and turn them into their shed, safe from wolves. Wolves do come near our houses, but always at night and never for long, because the dogs raise a terrible fuss. The men go out then and try to kill the wolves, so far without success, because the wolves are wary.

Travelers walking to Rivermouth don't come onto the Riverside. After they leave the valley below the Benchland, they follow a steep and difficult road close to the river. They pass directly below us, but not many realize we are so close. Coming here would lead them astray, because they would have to backtrack to reach the river road again. Downstream from us, the Riverside land ends against the rock wall, a half-day walk south and east of the houses.

MY HEART IS LIGHT this evening, for Kyle has returned. We gather with the entire group by two big fires of celebration on the bench, and everyone is excited. At their fire, the children squeal with delight, because Grandmother Folke is telling a story. She is the oldest of us, almost sixty, and I have enjoyed her stories all my life. I believe she invents each one as she tells it, but she denies it. She has a great talent, and when she is gone no one will be able to replace her.

We are celebrating a remarkable change in our fortunes. When the men returned from Rivermouth—Kyle, Father, and Brandr—they drove a bullock pulling a cart that rolls on wheels. We have intended for years to have a bullock cart once we were established on the Riverside. We will keep the bullock in a pen next to our goats, and in the same shed as the goats during winter. Bullocks are tough and smart—no easy prey for wolves. I hope we have him for years. We won't be able to bring the cart onto the Riverside, because the path is too narrow. We'll leave it nearby, somewhere not obvious, such as below the Benchland, behind a grove of trees at the base of the cliff.

In addition to the bullock cart, the men brought back woven woolen cloth. We talked this evening about how to use it. Woolen is lighter and warmer than hide and far easier to sew. We could use a great deal more. Next year, we will use the bullock cart to carry grain to Rivermouth for trade. That's why we wanted the cart. In the past, we have traded small valuable things—arrows with redmetal heads, bracelets, glarestone knives. Next summer we will trade grain for the first time. The bench grows enough grain to feed us all. Ours grown on the Riverside is for trade.

A sunny and encouraging plan. Our group is like a fruit tree beginning to bear. I must stop often and remind myself that enemies could cut it down.

WE SLEEP ON THE BENCHLAND—a holiday for the children, seeing friends they no longer live with. I visit the spirit chamber, where I ponder Uncle Sigurd's warning and what we can do to be ready. This problem dampens my spirit, because I love the Riverside and don't want to leave, but I must consider my children. So few of us live away from the bench that to protect ourselves against invasion seems impossible. And yet— if it were, Uncle Sigurd wouldn't have said to be ready, but to abandon the place and return to the bench. He must have known how we could prepare.

This truth is of the spirit.

I will understand better when Jered appears, because his coming must also be connected with Uncle Sigurd's warning. I am torn between patience and fear.

THEY SIT TOGETHER on the long flight, a man and a woman. He is tall and looks rugged and good humored in midlife; she is younger, slim, striking. Both are dark haired and dark eyed but have Nordic features, an odd similarity.

They sit in business class. Alys Engberg, formerly a minister of the Swedish government, is accustomed to traveling the world as a VIP and never flies coach. She is an only child, scion of an aristocratic family and the inheritor of modest wealth, a fact she keeps strictly to herself. Her companion is Jarrett Eriksson, cave photographer, recipient of many awards. He is co-author of Spirit Chamber, a book of photographs of a now-famous cave that was once home to a colony of Copper Age people. The book became a sensation when it was published, and its author is now as well known for his lectures as his photographs; he speaks often on cave photography and on Alice's Cave.

The relationship of the two travelers is not obvious. For much of the overwater portion of the flight, she sleeps while he looks at her, lost in thought. He married young but divorced years ago. He travels frequently, normally alone. What is he thinking? Perhaps simply trying to understand why fate has put him in the company of this woman.

At the first bloom of dawn, the North Sea is behind them and the lights of Denmark are visible ahead. Soon the flight will begin its descent toward Stockholm. Now he is the sleeper, she the watcher. The airplane is abruptly cold, and he huddles in his sleep. She reaches over and tucks a blanket around him.

STOCKHOLM IS BEAUTIFUL this Sunday morning—dignified and quiet. Alys's friend picks us up, a woman Alys has known for years through caving. Kristin Dahlquist is fascinating, a woman of God, a priest in the Lutheran-Episcopal Church of Sweden. Luckily for us, she is not working this Sunday. She takes us to her home, where I meet Joanie, her charming young American wife. Over a late breakfast we talk about Alice's Cave and *Spirit Chamber*. A copy of the book lies open on a coffee table in the living room.

Kristin's years-long fascination with the cave comes out as Alys and I talk about our experiences and plans. "Alys, will I *ever* get to see that cave?"

"It's difficult, Kristin. I told you our trip is against the rules. I would hate to see you defrocked for committing a crime."

"So my car can go, but I can't?"

This touches a nerve, and Alys gives up. "OK. I'll take you there, obviously not this trip. You and Joanie. But it must stop there. Too many people would increase the risk of discovery and would be bad for the cave."

WE LEAVE IN KRISTIN'S SUV. Alys drives, talking about how to retrieve her things from her apartment without tipping off the stalker, who often hangs out there. "I suspect he'll be at the airport at 9:30 tomorrow morning, when I was originally scheduled to arrive. We can grab my gear then. Once he realizes I'm not on the plane, he'll return to the apartment, but we'll need only a few minutes."

She takes us to the hotel, across the street from a park. "Everything we need is close. The apartment is right around the corner, so tomorrow morning will be simple."

I enjoy my tourist role. Alys approves of my jeans-based attire and stops in a store she likes, open on Sunday, to disguise herself as an American tourist. I see her in a new light; she *belongs* in this high-tone neighborhood. She is utterly familiar with the area. In the clothing store, she is greeted deferentially—in English, for my benefit—as "Madame Minister."

"I grew up right here when I was in Sweden. After my mother died I lived here full time, in my father's apartment, which is now mine. I went to high school in Fairfax County, Virginia, because my father thought I needed an American education. I went to Radcliffe and then came back to Stockholm University for a Masters."

"What was your Masters field?"

"Political Science, of course. If you'd known my father you wouldn't ask."

By this time we both fit the tourist model, down to the camera around my neck. Alys's long hair is down, which I haven't seen in public before. She is gorgeous, and I take tourist-like pictures of her. "It's smart to stay awake all day and to get some sun," she says. "It eases the jet lag." We have lunch in a little cafe and end up on a sunny bench in the park. I'm enjoying myself immensely.

"Let's put off buying supplies until tomorrow," she says, laughing. "We deserve a day off, and I'd like to show you Stockholm on a summer Sunday."

Stockholm is a city of islands, waterways, bridges, and parks, with monumental architecture everywhere. I shoot hundreds of pictures. By day's end, I'm tapped out with terminal jet lag, and we have a long day ahead of us tomorrow. Alys's tour ends in a little restaurant, where once again she is greeted with great respect, despite her tourist disguise.

"Alys, after today, I'm even more impressed that you flew to the US on Monday and were able to function normally. Don't you suffer jet lag?"

"I'm used to it. Short naps help, as long as you avoid frightening dreams. You're doing well, for an amateur. I loved showing you around my town."

MONDAY MORNING happens according to plan. We drive Kristin's car into the gated apartment garage and retrieve the caving gear from its garage closet. "I don't want to go into the apartment," Alys says. "I know it's not the way I left it. It will upset me. But I have to get some clothes."

The apartment is enormous and immaculate. It leaves me speechless. She gives me a brief tour. "My father, through and through. I would never have the place otherwise; the waiting lists are twenty years long." Her cleaning service did a good job of restoring order after the burglary, but she shows me where her computer used to be. She disappears into her bedroom and emerges in ten minutes with a packed duffel bag.

Half an hour later we tour the aisles in a big market, and an hour after that we head north. "Take me to Alice's Cave, driver," Alys says, as she curls up for a nap.

"Are we going up the river to that awful road? Or the very long mountain road west of the cave?"

"The river." She doesn't open her eyes. "The awful road is an advantage. It will deter others."

AN HOUR HASN'T PASSED when I first suspect we're being followed. A tan Jeep is always in view behind us, even though I vary the speed. I'm not convinced, but I'll tell Alys when she wakes up.

We reach the coast by three, with hours of driving still ahead. I'm awake, more or less, but my caffeine level is low, and in a small town I stop at a restaurant for a refill. Alys wakes instantly. "What?"

"Stopping for coffee. I think someone may be following us. Perhaps your pal."

"That's plausible. He could have staked out the apartment this morning and seen us. Nothing he does surprises me."

The tan Jeep goes by, headed north, and I point it out. "There he is. He'll wait for us somewhere north of here. Shall we try to lose him?"

"How? He knows where we're going."

"What does he want?"

"The police think he simply wants to remain close. He's stalking me because he's obsessed with me. They can't help unless he does something violent or illegal."

"We could stay here for the night and leave in the wee hours."

"Jarrett, I'm not going to reorganize my life because of him. Let's simply carry on. If he's following us, he is. Nothing about this trip was in my computer. He'll have to figure it out from go, and once we're in the cave, what can he do? He certainly won't be rappelling down that cliff. If I actually see him, I'll give him a piece of my mind. And in case he gets violent, I'm armed."

"You have a gun? Sweden allows that?"

"You can own any weapons you want, even automatic weapons and assault rifles. You can't normally carry them, but I have a carry permit because I was Culture Minister and had a stalker. The gun is in my duffel. I grabbed it out of the safe when I went in to get my clothes."

"I had no idea. Now you turn out to be Annie Oakley."

"You bet."

OUR COFFEE STOP expands into dinner. By the time we're through eating, Alys has come around to my point of view. We take adjoining rooms in a small hotel and park the car in a closed garage. We see no sign of the Jeep.

In my room, I email Mira with an update on our progress. I have a reply within minutes.

From: kramnick@johnshopkins.edu
To: jarrett@erikssonphoto.com
Date: Mon Jul 9 12:30 PM EDT
Subj: You're dreaming

What could you find in the cave that will head off whatever danger you saw in your dream? What do you think your trip will accomplish? We wish you the best, but - with respect to the power of the spirit chamber - we think you're heading for a dead end. Sometimes a dream is just a dream.

R&M

Keep us posted. We fly Friday. I'll see you Saturday AM.

She has gone too far.

I have been so steadfast, always there for her. I deserve better. A man has to keep his dignity. She must pay for this.

I always suspected there was another man, when she traveled so often. Oh, she was clever. She made sure she was always alone when I saw her. But she didn't fool me. She didn't even make much of an effort to disguise the elaborate schedules. I tried to tell myself she could be traveling for her job. But my inner voice kept telling me there was another man.

I had to know, so I decided to follow her.

While she was gone, I let myself into her apartment. She is *terribly* careless about her door code. It was the most beautiful apartment I ever saw, and her smell was everywhere. I knew there would be no evidence—she's too crafty for that—but I looked anyway. Everywhere. Found nothing.

I took her computer. I took it home and found her travel schedule, and I followed her. To the US, to Washington. I didn't know where she was, so I watched her room. It was empty for two nights. Then she appeared, early in the morning, and I didn't lose her again. She caught a train later that day, and I followed. A man picked her up, and I followed. They went to a restaurant.

And then to his apartment. She stayed in his apartment. Brazen harlot.

He is the other man. He is obviously American. He too must pay.

TUESDAY 10 JULY

She brought him back to Stockholm! They are together right now!

She was supposed to arrive in London on Sunday. She was not on the plane. I came back to her apartment and waited for her. She is clever, though: she came to the apartment Monday, exactly when her original flight was scheduled to arrive. She was with HIM. In HIS car. Where were they Sunday night? In some hotel, probably. She has no shame.

When they left, I followed them. They stopped for the night. In another hotel.

The only place they could possibly be going is the cave. They'll go to the top of the mountain, where she went before.

Once they get there, they'll go down into the cave for days. That will give me time. I'll have to think about what to do.

YRSA IS NINE, and she says she knew the spirit before she was born. "Yrsa will be the greatest of our healers," Aunt Inge said. "She will surprise us all." She has already done that many times, beginning with finding Hargard.

Yrsa was only two when we first realized she wanted to go into the pool in the spirit chamber. I couldn't imagine why. The water is cold, and the rocks are slippery. I love the spirit chamber beyond anything, but I have never had any desire to go into that water. Not so Yrsa; she strained toward the far side of the pool, where the water is deep and dark. "Hargard," she said. "Spirit." She would not be dissuaded. On every visit, she jumped into the water and paddled as hard as her two-year-old self could, spluttering and splashing, until she was so cold we had to dry her by the fire. Every time, the first thing she said was, "Go back."

I never worried about her, because she was always within reach. Mother or I stood in that freezing water, close enough to grab her.

She was four when she found what she had been seeking, and I have never been so terrified. We had taken her to the spirit chamber, where she was splashing around as usual. Mother was in the pool with her, because I was pregnant. Then Yrsa disappeared. In an instant. The splashing stopped, and in the firelight we saw only the ripples where she had been. Mother was right there. She reached under the water everywhere. No little girl.

Yrsa was gone much too long. She could never have held her breath all that time. I felt as if my heart had been torn out.

Everything happened so quickly that in memory it seems no time passed at all. Yrsa reappeared, shivering and blue with cold. Mother swept her up and brought her to the fire and a warm wrap. Yrsa was excited and tried to tell us why, but she was too cold to speak.

I could still hardly breathe. I held her on my lap and cried.

Eventually, teeth chattering, she said, "I found it!"

"Found what, Yrsa?"

"Hargard! Right there!" She pointed toward the rock wall on the far side of the pool.

Mother and I looked at each other, mystified.

Yrsa insisted that I carry her into the pool and wade over to the other side. When we got there—the water was above my waist—she pulled my arm under. "Feel *here!*"

The rock wall didn't reach to the bottom. It ended a handspan below the surface.

"Hargard! On the other side! Go under! Take me there! I have to go back! Don't you *feel* it?"

I was already cold.

"Yrsa, let me warm up first, and then I'll try it. By myself at first." We left the pool to sit by the fire, and I looked in wonder at the place I knew so well. Had Mother and I both missed something important?

When I could put it off no longer, I waded into the water—alone, over Yrsa's protests. I stood where the wall ended below the surface, took a deep breath, and ducked under.

I PULLED MYSELF OUT OF THE WATER onto a rocky surface in total darkness. From the sound of the stream, I knew I was no longer in the spirit chamber. I could not explore in the dark, so I simply sat there listening. I heard the stream splash down a hole. I've wondered all my life how it gets from the spirit chamber into the living chamber. Now I know.

And the spirit! It engulfed me. I was cold, but it warmed me. I sat there with spirit song in my ears and fell into a kind of trance. I knew truths I had only suspected before. I had never guessed at such a place. Yrsa had to show me.

I was reluctant to leave, but I knew I had to go back to the real world and the warmth of the fire.

Then a small hand grabbed my leg, and Yrsa pulled herself out of the water and onto my lap. "Mother, I told you. The spirit lives here. It called to me."

THAT HAPPENED FIVE YEARS AGO, and now when Yrsa wants to go to the spirit chamber, she means Hargard. The day after that first visit, Mother and I—with Yrsa, of course—brought wood and fire tools in greased hide bags. We built a fire and warmed ourselves as we saw the domain of the spirit for the first time—a small room with no visible ceiling, only an opening rising into blackness. Stream sound filled the place, and the walls glistened in the firelight.

Since then Yrsa and I have returned many times, always bringing wood for a fire. Mother joins us, but not often. We sleep there sometimes, and the dreams are unlike any other, but sleeping or not, on every visit I enter a dreamlike reality. I see the cave in an earlier time, before people. I speak to Grandfather and Aunt Inge and the other lost elders. The experiences are crystalline and leave vivid memories, because I live them.

Hargard. Where time stops.

MORNING SUN slants over the sea to dazzle mind and eye—lovely, but at an ungodly hour, a gift of the far north, where full dark is unknown in summer. Alys and I finish breakfast and head north before seven despite my spending a half hour shooting early-morning scenery. I feel less jet lagged, nearly human. She drives, and I divide my time between admiring the green coastal scenery and thinking about what we're doing.

I'm returning to the cave at last, but hardly by choice. Alice's Cave is summoning me, in dreams but also in reality, by thrusting Alys Engberg into my life. Two weeks ago, today's scene would have been beyond my imagining.

The cave is more than a destination; it is a force. Whatever the nature of the spirit chamber, it has power enough to have brought me into contact with the original people. It feels benign, that power, but beyond ken. And I am about to meet it again. At its behest. Does it have a reason?

Will I see Alice? I assume so, otherwise the rash of recent occurrences is impossible to explain—the dreams, Alys's experiences, Mira's new findings.

I see other complications. What does it mean that for a companion I have this astonishing woman? Accomplished, cultured, beautiful—but related to me *how*? I was relieved when she plainly said she did not want us to be involved—but in the spirit chamber, will we have any choice in the matter? I feel my single status at risk.

"A penny for your thoughts, Mr. Photographer." The first words in some time. "Let me guess. You wonder what task awaits us."

"Something like that. I've been reviewing the bidding, and the only thing clear is that I'm a simple-minded working man ill-suited to dealing with matters of the spirit. I'm beyond my depth. Why do you say task? Can't we simply be tourists?"

"You say this? You who have touched a person across the ages? You who have seen an ancient funeral ceremony? Were you a tourist then? In this game we are all players. You and I have a task. I'm sure of it."

WE STOP FOR AN EARLY LUNCH in Rivermouth and reach the top of the mountain by four. We never see the tan Jeep; perhaps it was not Alys's stalker after all.

Everything looks exactly as it did fourteen years ago, when I camped on this mountaintop with Roger and Mira. The sky is dotted with fluffy clouds that cast seductive shadows onto the hills around. The river flows toward the shelf from the north but then curves eastward toward Rivermouth and the sea. This is the highest mountain in the area, and we can see miles of river canyon in both directions. Another expansive landscape stretches into the west, eventually to higher mountains. To the south, the hills descend for miles in rolling waves. I have a pang of regret for selling this land.

We will leave the car where it is for now and sleep near it tonight before we descend the deep pit tomorrow morning. An outdoor camp is far more comfortable than a cave bivouac. Today we will rig the two drops—to the upper entrance and down the big pit.

We loop our rope around a huge boulder at the cliff edge. I'm pleased that our rigging is not obvious. The rappel is short and easy, not quite vertical. It leaves us on the ledge outside the entrance. The passage from there to the lip of the pit is a climb into darkness that banishes my jet lag at last. I'm caving, and I feel fine. We see side passages; there is no end to the complexity of this cave.

The view into the pit from its lip is intimidating. It feels positively dangerous. "We should call it Alys's Deep," I say. "You did this alone? Twice? I'm impressed."

We take some time to rig the drop. The pit is a narrow east-west slot at the top but flares out immediately. We have many choices of boulders and cave formations for our primary belay. Alys advises using the west edge to position the rope above the mid-pit ledge she found.

We double-check our rigging and return to the upper entrance, where it is still broad daylight at 8:30. Sunset, or what passes for it here, will be about 10:30.

A surprise—Alys secretly stowed elegant packaged dinners from her local deli, along with a bottle of wine. We camp on the hilltop with views of forever.

OUR DAY BEGINS EARLY. We eat luxuriously for breakfast—eggs, bacon, fresh juice.

Alys looks at me. "Must we camp at the car every night? Would it be so bad to sleep in the spirit chamber, if we leave no trace?"

"Let's take the bivouac gear and decide later."

I drive Kristin's car into the trees and tarp it. We are ready to descend before six, and by seven we stand in darkness at the lip of Alys's Deep.

Alys descends first, without a pack. I lower our two caving packs and two bags of gear to her one at a time and then begin my own descent. I'm cautious—in the darkness I can see only the flare of Alys's light two hundred feet below, and the rocks are unrelenting. The top of the descent is vertical, through space; the dome is shaped like an inverted bell. Lower, the walls are closer. I step onto the ledge beside Alys without difficulty. The rope continues down to the spirit chamber.

I remove my harness and take some time to adjust it. Alys explores the area.

"Jarrett, look! I didn't see this before."

She has found a hidden side passage—horizontal, level, walking height. It leads into the unknown, and I find it hard to resist. Even after a summer-long survey, I hardly know this cave. We won't pursue this lead now— the spirit chamber calls—but we won't forget it.

Another half hour brings us and our gear to the bottom of the pit, a hundred feet below the ledge. I recognize the place; Roger and I surveyed the short climb from the spirit chamber to this spot. We looked up into the dark abyss overhead, shook our heads at its vertical walls that offered not the slightest fingerhold, and accepted it as an unclimbable mystery. We placed a tape flag to mark the station and pressed on with our survey. I show Alys the flag, which could have been placed this morning.

It's silent here, but I hear the stream as soon as we start down the passage, and shortly after that we enter the spirit chamber at its narrow western end, well upstream from the pool.

In that instant, the entire adventure becomes real. Fifteen minutes later we stand in the place where the impossible happened, on Alice's flowstone.

CAVES CALM BY THEIR CONSTANCY. When I first came to the spirit chamber, its beauty and presence awed me. I stand here surrounded by the spirit of the place, and as I listen to the stream I am once again spellbound. On a whim, I record stream song on my phone. Perhaps it will be good enough to play in my living room.

I met Alice here and saw a funeral ceremony here, but what comes first to mind is the peace the place imparts. Sleeping on this flowstone saved me during that stressful summer.

Alys is seated, eyes closed in her absorption. She looks very much like Alice and her mother, and I am captivated by the idea that she is descended from them. I shoot a dozen photographs. I have thousands of spirit chamber images, but these are the first that contain Alys Engberg, who looks as if she had been born here.

Eventually we stand and stretch and move to the living chamber, where Mira's red tape pathways reflect the light from the gated entry door—much more light than we saw in the summer of exploration, when a small mountain of rock blocked the entry. We tour the walls to look at the paintings, clockwise starting at the entrance, earliest pictures first. We see the two founding couples as young explorers, as young parents, as grandparents in a substantial colony. I know all these images, but the paintings have a fresh reality my photographs do not. We examine the four hearths. Alice knew this hall with only two, and each of us has seen it that way.

We stand inside the locked gate and stare out at the distant sea.

"Like prisoners looking through the bars," Alys muses.

"If it weren't for our rope, we would be."

"I'D LOVE TO SEE MORE of the cave." Alys sounds wistful. "I know very little of it."

"It's Tuesday night. We have a few days before Roger and Mira arrive. Where should we start?"

"I've waited for years to see the cave with you as a guide. You tell me what I want to see. The ancient western entrance, for example, with its pit? The tablets? Somewhere in this cave I expect to discover something about myself."

"Let's begin with Mira's connection to the cave near the river. That will be new to me too."

We eat cold caver chow in the living chamber, tacitly avoiding taking food into the spirit chamber. We spend the night camped there, though, well upstream. I dream of the pool glowing from a light source we cannot see.

IN THE LARGE WESTERN CHAMBER, we study the map Mira sent—a photo of another of Alice's tablets, free of crazing. Even with map in hand, we have to search at length for the connecting passage, because the entry is well hidden between parallel slabs of stone. I am not surprised Roger and I missed it.

We squeeze between the entry slabs and emerge onto a balcony overlooking a floor far below us. Rigging the descent is simple, and a half hour later we stand at the bottom. A single large borehole passage leads downward and southeast. We set out walking.

Alice's map of this passage is detailed and exact; it shows each turn. She would have made a fine cave surveyor. The passage descends steadily but remains easy and goes on for some distance—nearly a mile, we think. The ceiling is spectacular, with soda straws and many other small formations.

On the map, the passage leads to an exit near the river, but we come to a dead end where the cave is blocked by breakdown. The exit Alice used no longer exists. What we find in its place becomes the focus of our visit.

Paintings. Huge, dramatic paintings.

A BLOODY BATTLE rages outside this cave, near four houses we know from Alice's tablets. The paintings in the living chamber are three or four feet square. These three scenes are enormous—nearly six feet tall and twice as long. They cover both walls of the passage.

They are obviously Alice's work.

The detail is staggering. "Her magnum opus," Alys says. "Look—she has small figures in the background and large ones in the foreground. Perspective. Silly me. I had the preposterous notion, instilled by an Ivy League citadel of higher learning, that the Greeks were the first to develop perspective representations. Either Alice was extremely precocious or I misunderstood."

The paintings show the houses under attack by a large force, which is gathered upstream in the first painting, assaulting the area near the houses in the second, and fleeing in tatters in the third. We walk from scene to scene to take it all in.

The houses are protected by a tall defense wall made of tree trunks. Alys stares. "That wall decided matters. What a job, to cut those trunks, haul them, and erect them."

"They had to drag them. They didn't have the wheel."

We separate again, contemplating details as people do at a museum display of a huge painting. We have almost thirty feet of paintings to examine.

"You should see this, Jarrett." Alys is looking at a smaller fourth painting, showing a tree trunk being moved. It has been cut to length—perhaps fifteen feet—and stripped of limbs. A dozen men support the light end. The heavy end rests on a sturdy oxcart pulled by a single ox led by one man.

Alice's people had the wheel.

I already have my camera out. "This will stun Mira. Wheels! The first evidence."

Alys examines details while I shoot. "The wall is too tall for the attackers to climb. It forces them to walk along its whole length while archers shoot at them through holes."

When I finish the photos, we stand back and look at the paintings as a group. I am astonished by their extent. These walls have a lot of paint. "Alys, she must have painted these when she was young. An older woman wouldn't have the energy for such a project."

Alys looks at the paintings under LED light. "These are much more weathered than the paintings in the living chamber. They must have spent a long time exposed to outside air."

"We'll bring Roger and Mira here, first thing."

"I HARDLY KNOW what to do next," Alys says. "I'm puzzled. This is all deeply satisfying, but I was sure I would find some definite connection between me and this cave. I wonder what I expected?"

"We've seen no sign of Alice. Of course, we haven't seen anything like the whole cave."

She completes my thought. "But we slept in the spirit chamber, which is where we would expect to see her. Perhaps we should return there."

"We also have your passage to check out, from the ledge."

We retrace our route and ascend our downrope to reach the balcony. I check out the walls on the way up.

Without a rope in place, this climb would be scary and dangerous; perhaps Alice's people discovered it from above. We leave our rigging in place. We'll be back.

From the balcony we squeeze back into the main cave and head for the bottom of Alys's Deep. We climb our rope to the mid-pit ledge and take a moment to enjoy the place. The ledge protrudes into the pit like a high balcony with no rail, looking over an immense darkness. No photo can convey the feeling, because photos catch only a single moment, normally well lighted. From the ledge I see only our roving flashlight beams that light now the wall across the pit, now the dizzy space below us, now an interesting formation. Our brains can't accurately combine those moments; we visualize the space as far bigger than it is. In a cave tour, the room shrinks when the lights come on. Darkness makes hearing more acute, and echoes often help me visualize, but not here; this pit is too big for that, reaching two hundred feet up and a hundred down, and our every sound comes back to us from many directions.

ALYS'S SIDE LEAD is a downclimb between projecting rock structures that look like mythical dragons defending the lair where the gold is hidden. I'm surprised she saw it.

We lower our gear and squeeze down into a standing-height passage. It runs a few hundred feet level, headed north, crossing over the top of the spirit chamber. We pass a junction that curves around to the west—another lead to check out later.

Our comfortable route soon becomes a stoopway. Beyond that we have to crawl. We drop to our bellies and push our packs before us, fearing that the passage will pinch off. I am relieved when it opens out onto a tiny ledge at the top of still another pit dropping into the dark unknown.

My flashlight catches a glint of water below, and without warning I have an attack of—what? Nerves? Fear?

We rig a downrope over a stalagmite the size of a fire hydrant, and I go first. The glint of water comes from a pool, the main feature of a small room with no obvious exit. I descend slowly, more and more nervous. My heart pounds as I land, and as I call, "Off rope," my voice shakes.

What am I afraid of?

I SEE THE DIM GLOW of the fire when I turn, and two figures beside it—a woman and a girl. Perhaps they had been lying down; now they stand. I know Alice immediately even though I last saw her as a child. I swivel my headlamp upward to avoid blinding her, and she meets my eyes with the look I remember so well. Her adult self is all but a double of Alys. Alice is somewhat the smaller of the two, but they are like twins.

My eye falls on the child, a girl of eight or nine. She looks into me, through me, seeing everything. She leans to her mother and whispers, and Alice laughs quietly.

When Alys arrives and stands beside me, the questions are resolved, the ones that have played around the edges of my mind. The two women are surely related, but they are different people. I can see them both.

My mind struggles to comprehend. Alice and her daughter are not ethereal figures. They are here as much as I. I'm wide awake, but this reality has the texture of a dream, of otherness. I know I am in the ancient time, because Alice stands before me. If I were to visit the living chamber, the entrance would lead directly onto the shelf, with no gate, no mountain of rock. Still, I remain in the modern time. My rappel harness has modern fittings, and my pack holds a camera.

My camera. What would happen if I took a picture?

This place is like nothing in my experience. Perhaps it has induced a trance state. Or maybe reality is more complex than I have realized.

THE TWO WOMEN STARE AT EACH OTHER, taken by their similarity, and when Alys removes her helmet and her hair spills out, the resemblance only grows. We stand as a group of four, not knowing what to do next.

The little girl settles it. She holds out both hands, palm up, one toward her mother, the other toward Alys.

Alice hovers her right hand an inch above her daughter's, palm down, and then turns to me and extends the other hand.

We are acting out a script that has been in place forever.

I meet Alice's hand and extend my left hand toward Alys, who has been watching, astonished. I can read her thoughts: what is about to happen? Unsure but not afraid, she sets her helmet down and hovers her hand over mine. I feel her living energy.

Alys turns toward the girl, who remains standing with her right hand out. From the moment their eyes lock, I feel electricity. Alys extends a hand to her, and our circle closes.

I am stunned by a surge of power that sweeps through me—through us all. We are one, we four.

The girl looks at me as her mother once did. Abruptly, fire flares up around us, and I realize that no, I am not out of my mind, but for the first time know myself completely, here among my people.

THURSDAY 12 JULY, EARLY MORNING

There is no escape. They are everywhere, those who do government surveillance. Before I came to Sweden I thought the problem was limited to the US. I was delighted when I found out she was Sweden's Minister of Culture, because I had lost her for a few years. I took a job in Sweden and moved to Stockholm, but the surveillance only got worse. They spy on me with microwaves and lasers and high-energy radio waves, not to speak of the rays emanated by a new secret technology only they have. They spy on me through my phone and my electric wires. They listen to every phone call. They photograph me whenever I leave the house. If I buy a computer, they manage to have it altered before I take delivery, and it reports on me.

Don't think it can't happen to you. This is the age of big brother.

I was lucky to discover by accident that black clothes block the secret new rays and reduce the pain of microwave radiation. I had to find that out myself. It is tightly-controlled classified information. Very few know about it.

Now the surveillance has cost me two days. My time means nothing to them. They attacked me in my hotel room with microwaves of a new type, which pass through even my black shirt and jeans. All day yesterday the attack was relentless. I curled up in terrible pain like an ant being cooked by a malicious child with a magnifier. When the pain finally let up last night I was too exhausted to move.

Two days! I could have lost her again. She could have gone into the cave Tuesday and left already. But I carry on.

Thursday 12 July, afternoon

I did not lose her.

They are together, the seducer and the faithless harlot. In the cave.

I found their car. They thought it was well hidden, but I found it. And I found their rappel rope.

This trip, I have my cave gear. It has been years, but you never forget. I strap on my old harness and use my rappel rack—both from the caving club where I met her. The descent terrifies me, and I cannot look down, but the rope leads me to a cave entrance, as I knew it would. I lost my helmet years ago, but I have flashlights. I walk through the entrance and climb a slope to a ledge over a deep hole. Nothing below. My flashlight isn't bright enough to show me the bottom. I drop a pebble and listen carefully. Nothing.

A feeling of dread and terror comes out of that hole. A soul-eating monster lives there, huge and pitiless.

A rappel rope goes into that pit. No way could I go down there, but she will never be safe from me now that she has betrayed me so cruelly.

They will have to come back up that rope.

I take my pocketknife and cut a few strands. It will serve her right to fall. I hope she climbs first. He will have to look at her broken body.

I cut through more of the rope. I must take care. Too much, and she will fall immediately and not be hurt. Too little, and she won't fall at all.

I cut a few more strands.

JERED IS ONE OF US! I suspected it long ago. His wife too. She looks very much like me. Could she be descended from me? Later Yrsa tells me they both are. Also that she is not yet his wife but will be in time. Yrsa surely knew what would happen when she drew us together. Did she know the fire would rise around us?

We stand in a circle, as she intended, joined by the spirit. The fire has already subsided. Of course I think of Aunt Inge, who was married in a ring of fire, and I remember that she called Yrsa a child of fire.

I turn to him. "Jered."

"Alys!" His face crinkles into a smile. Our languages are different, but names are names.

His wife looks into my eyes, and I know without being told that she is another Alys. Her face is wet with tears, and for no reason I begin crying too.

I break the contact to hug Yrsa to me and say her name. Jered's wife—I will call her Alys, but it feels strange—smiles and repeats, "Yrsa."

Yrsa whispers, "Mother, she is like you." Then, looking at all of us, she opens her arms to take in the room. "Hargard."

I knew Jered was coming, but I had no hint of this spirit union. The four of us, joined forever. In Hargard. With a ring of fire.

I LEARN MANY THINGS in our moments of contact. Jered and Alys have come for a purpose.

"Mother," Yrsa says, "we must see the Riverside Cave. They will understand." Without hesitation, she jumps into the pool and disappears under the wall. I smile once more at Jered and his wife and follow Yrsa.

In the spirit chamber, we change into dry clothes, light torches, and start upstream.

Why must we go to the Riverside?

When we reach the top of the descent down into the Riverside Cave, I am surprised to see that our hempen rope—the one we climbed only a few hours ago—has been replaced with a rope that is obviously Jered's. Thinner than ours, and softer, without bristles.

Yrsa is not surprised. She knows we are in Jered's time.

Yrsa starts down the rope in the dark, as she always does. I follow, and we find ourselves in the familiar

Riverside Cave. As we walk its length, I am more and more puzzled about why I must come to this place I know so well.

SOMETHING IS WRONG. After the final turn, I cannot see the light at the exit as usual. We walk in silence, and I am afraid, for I have never seen such darkness here. The area inside the entrance is usually alive with birds and bats. Today, the cave is silent and dead.

I remind myself that we came from Hargard into Jered's time.

I see why there is no light. A mountain of rock blocks the exit and spills fifty paces up into the cave. We cannot reach the exit; we will have to turn back.

As we do, I look at the walls and understand the reason for coming here.

Paintings! Large pictures on the wall. They look like mine.

I have never made paintings here.

When I was eleven, I dreamed of Jered showing me a tablet I had not made yet, of Kyle and me with Yrsa. Once again, through the spirit, I am looking at scenes from the future. But this time I am wide awake.

WHAT THESE PAINTINGS SHOW shakes me—the Riverside is under attack, as Uncle Sigurd feared. I see our four houses, but also a fortress wall made of tree trunks standing in a tight row between the houses and the bank that drops to the river. The wall makes the path onto the Riverside long and narrow. Anyone coming here must walk its entire length.

In the first picture, an army of black-haired men is gathered along the river, below the Benchland. It seems to be sunset; atop the mountain above the bench, the sun lights men pointing at the attackers. Our lookouts!

The second shows an awful scene. It is early morning, and a mob of attackers storms the Riverside, running behind the fortress wall, single file. On our side of the wall, more than a dozen hunters shoot through gaps—arrow slits. Hundreds of arrows are stacked and ready. The attack is failing; not many enemies survive to enter the Riverside. The painting shows two who do emerge onto the open area in front of the houses, but many people shoot at them. Outside the wall, bodies lie everywhere.

The third painting shows the surviving attackers heading upriver through the valley, about midmorning. Not many remain. Not half.

In a smaller fourth painting, men use the bullock cart to move tree trunks to the wall.

The paintings show what lies ahead and what we must do to survive. I will have to study them closely.

WHEN YRSA AND I LEFT THE HOUSE this morning, she climbed briefly on the six posts lying near the cave entrance—the posts for the new house. Each of them is as thick as a man's thigh. The men felled the trees near the river and limbed them and cut them to length where they fell. The bullock cart made the cut posts easy to carry, but it couldn't come all the way onto the Riverside, so they had to be dragged the rest of the way.

Cutting and moving each of those posts took two full days with five men working. The painting of the wall shows almost forty posts. Thinking of what we must do overwhelms me. Every man and boy will have to help.

The paintings show only four houses, but the new posts don't appear; they must be part of the fortress wall. That means we will build the wall this year. The shadows and sunlight in the paintings look like summer's end, and we are already beyond midsummer. We have a scant two months.

My mind races as I consider the details. The wall has posts of different lengths and thicknesses, because the slits for shooting occur at several heights. Inside the wall, smaller logs run its length, at different levels, and each one is tied to every post with hemp.

"Yrsa, I must draw plans for the wall. Help me remember exactly where it is, how long, and how high. Every detail."

Yrsa understands. She remembers Uncle Sigurd's warning.

"MY GOD, JARRETT." In three words Alys says it all.

She is shaken, and I can understand; I had at least met Alice before. "The fire around us—did that really happen?"

"I felt the heat. This place is its own reality."

We look at each other, struggling to process what happened.

WE ARE ALONE. Alice and Yrsa left abruptly, and we both know why: during the time of closeness, we learned that Alice was concerned about a possible attack. They learned they must visit the lower cave.

We decompress in silence until Alys says, "This is why we came."

"To show her the paintings? Or because this is your connection to your past?"

"Both. This *is* my past. I feel like one of them."

I SHINE A LIGHT into the pool. "Look. The wall ends a few inches down. This room adjoins the spirit chamber. That's how they get here. I wonder how they found it?"

"Yrsa found it. That little girl's wisdom is beyond me. She and I bonded, and I understood a great deal from her. This is *her* room. She named it."

"Hargard. And she brought us into the circle. Did she know what would happen?"

"What happened was a test of kinship. We passed."

"What does that mean? What now?"

Alys gives me the look. "Jarrett, I am in no condition to think. My beliefs and my understanding of the world have been shaken off their foundations. I am not the same person."

I WOULD LIKE TO STAY LONGER—much longer—but life outside beckons. "It's Thursday. Roger and Mira fly tomorrow. To meet them at the airport early Saturday, we need to leave today. We can stay at a local hotel and drive to Stockholm tomorrow."

"I'd like more time here."

"Me too. We'll be back. We need time away from the cave to process what happened. Also showers and real food."

We break the ascenders out of the packs and climb, Alys first. At the top, over a lunch of energy bars, I voice my puzzlement. "They could never get here without rigging. But think about the pool in the spirit chamber. At the far wall, it looks deep and eerie, with no hint of what lies beyond. And the water is freezing. How did Yrsa find the connection?"

"Hargard called to her, Jarrett."

THE RETURN TO ALYS'S DEEP begins with a tight crawl but softens quickly into a stoopway and then walking passage. We reach the westbound junction we saw— when? In another time, before Alice and Yrsa? In those two hours I've lived in a different world.

The side passage is interesting and difficult, with climbing and squeezing. It leads to a gallery overlooking an enormous pit—Alys's Deep. We are somewhere between the top and the mid-pit ledge. Far across the pit, we can see our rope. We have spent the last few hours in smaller spaces. The sheer volume around us gives Alys's Deep great majesty.

"Dead end," Alys says. "Interesting, though. A different perspective. The pit looks even scarier from here."

We return to the mid-pit ledge without difficulty. I have my pack off and am ready to buckle on ascenders when Alys intervenes. "Jarrett, we have time to visit the spirit chamber before we leave. I'd like to see Yrsa's water connection."

We strap on harnesses and rappel racks. Always nervous before a descent, I test-tug the rope.

Alys goes first. "On rope."

She slips off the edge. I lean over to watch but quickly feel dizzy and give up.

Perhaps twenty seconds later I hear a shriek of fear. Rope rushes by me. I reach for it, hoping to belay her, but too late. From below comes a crunching thud, and I am left with a length of slack rope in my hands.

Then silence.

I BEGIN BY SKETCHING the images on a hide, using charred sticks I find in the living chamber. Memory is fleeting. How many attackers did I see? How were the posts arranged? I work quickly because I feel time passing. The paintings give us advance warning, but how much?

I produce reasonable drawings—crude, but that's not important. As soon as I finish, Yrsa and I seek out Mother. The sun is low, and the day has been long and tiring, especially for Yrsa, but she knows we have no time to lose.

We find Mother and Father in their shelter. The spirit chamber is the best place for important discussions, but they must see the hide, and time is short, so Yrsa and I invite ourselves into their sanctuary.

They always greet Yrsa with joy. She is their first grandchild and as special to them as to me. They are old in Yrsa's eyes, but I still see them as the young couple I remember from my earliest days. Mother was not yet sixteen when I was born. Now she is over forty, and Father is older still.

I spread the hide on the shelter floor. Mother and Father glance quickly at the sketches and then examine them carefully. I don't need to explain. The images clearly show the Riverside under attack.

Mother turns to Yrsa and me. "Alys, did you see this in a dream? Is Jered involved?"

"Grandmother," Yrsa squeals, "I met him, in Hargard! I love him! And his wife! Her name is Alys too, and she looks exactly like Mother!" Yrsa puts her hand almost against mine. "The four of us made a circle like this, and the spirit joined us with fire. Mother and I learned that we had to go to the Riverside Cave right away, and when we did, we couldn't get out to our house, because the cave exit was blocked off by big rocks. But we saw these pictures on the walls."

Mother and Father are speechless.

Yrsa sees their puzzlement and explains. "The pictures aren't really there now. Mother will paint them later this year."

"*This* year?" Father sounds surprised. "How do you know? Why not next year, or the year after?"

I knew he would ask. "If the attack were next year, the paintings would show five houses. I think the posts for the fifth house are part of the wall."

Father and Mother sit silently, studying the sketches. I can almost see Mother's thought process. She realizes how much we must do. And she is our leader.

"Uncle Sigurd warned us an attack might come soon," she says. "Olaf, you'll have to take his place and lead the fighting. Druian will resent that, but it must be, and he will be in charge of building the wall. All of us will have to make arrows."

"A wall like that is a good solution," Father says. "I wonder who had the idea originally?"

"Grandfather, don't you *see*? It comes from the spirit!"

"And from Uncle Sigurd," Mother says.

MOTHER AND I seek out Grandmother Folke to ask her help in telling everyone on the bench that we must meet tonight. Astrid is watching her children and my two little ones, but her husband—my cousin Soren, Aunt Angela's son—is here on the bench this afternoon, and he can tell everyone on the Riverside. We find him at the men's work area. He has taken over much of Grandfather and Uncle Sigurd's redmetal work.

"Aunt Ana! Alys! Yrsa!" He has been cleaning out the oven, and he is black all over.

"Soren," Mother says, "we need to meet tonight, with the entire group. Can you please go to the Riverside and tell everyone?"

He raises his eyebrows. "What reason should I give them?"

Mother looks steadily at him. "Tell them the meeting is about our survival."

I STARE INTO THE BLACKNESS without comprehension. What happened? Did the belay fail at the top? Impossible. My mind races. My ears ring. I cannot think.

Quickly enough, my caving reflexes cut in. I must reach Alys, and seconds could make the difference. Thank God I have plenty of rope. I belay a new downrope to a large formation. I test it thoroughly and start down, looking below as I rappel.

Before I reach the bottom, I see her lying on her side, covered in coils of rope. She looks broken. She could have fallen ten feet, or twenty—probably survivable, with luck—or eighty. Her pack, which was hanging below her, is a short distance away.

"Alys?"

No answer.

I unclip and bend over her. ABC—airway, breathing, circulation. She is breathing, although it seems rapid and shallow. She is covered with blood. I see nasty cuts on her face, arms, and head. Her left leg is doubled under her, obviously broken. Her helmet is cracked almost in half. My stomach twists as I remember that helmet from our first meeting.

Her pulse is 140. I inventory the cuts quickly. One on the side of her head is bleeding heavily, but I don't see any pumping arterial blood. I must not move her, at least not yet; she could have a spinal injury. I hope the leg took the damage and saved her spine. Find her jacket. Remove her helmet. Slip jacket under head. Emergency blanket; already she is cold and sweating. Shock will be a serious problem. I try to work carefully, but I am shaking.

I set her helmet to the side with the light still on to provide general illumination. I lay my pack open beside her and find alcohol, cotton, and gauze so I can work on the cuts, starting with the head gash, which is three inches long and still bleeding profusely. I use water from my bottles to sponge her bloody head and ear. I have to cut away some hair. I swab the cut with alcohol, apply antibiotic ointment, close the gash with butterfly strips, cover it with gauze as a compress, tape it down.

My heart is racing out of control, but Alys's pulse rate is 125, and her respiration is down to 40. She has shock symptoms—her forehead is clammy. And she remains unconscious.

Her caving suit is torn over the left shoulder, exposing another nasty gash. I cut the suit away and start to work. She whimpers and rolls to her back, wincing in pain when she moves her leg. She quickly subsides into unconsciousness, but I am relieved; I now suspect her spine is intact.

This cut is deep and ragged. It will require many stitches. Mop with alcohol. Antibiotic. Butterfly bandages. Compress. Tape. I need to treat many more cuts, some severe, but first I want to put her onto something softer. I find a foam bivouac mattress in her pack and gently work her onto it.

Alys shows no further sign of consciousness, but her pulse is down to 110. How long ago did she fall? Half an hour? I fought panic at first, but I'm beyond that. I gather the fallen rope and coil it, seeking the broken end. If it's frayed, I will conclude I caused the fall by leading the rope over a surface it couldn't tolerate. If the end is intact, it will mean my belay failed.

What I find is worse than either. The broken end has been cut almost through. It tore at the last, but the cut fibers are obvious.

The stalker. The police were wrong. He *is* dangerous.

I know disasters unfold in layers, and now that I have time to think ahead, I am afraid. How will I get Alys out? The original people knew of the upper entrance, but I have no idea how they reached it. The main entrance is gated. And I certainly can't leave Alys in her current condition.

We are trapped.

YRSA AND I STAY FOR A MEAL with Mother and Father. The two hearths outside are shared between all the shelters. Mother often cooks for a large group, but tonight we have only the four of us, which I think Yrsa prefers. Later, when the moon is high, Mother will tell the group about the paintings and the fortress wall. The little children will be asleep by then, curled up together in the cave. We will have about sixty-five adults and older children.

After we eat, Father is outside talking with other men, and Yrsa leaves us to look for her friends. I tell Mother about her part in our meeting with Jered and Alys in Hargard.

"Alys, she said the spirit joined you with fire. What did she mean?"

"When we made a circle, a ring of fire surrounded us, out of nowhere. It reminded me of Aunt Inge's painting of her wedding."

Mother closes her eyes. "I was on her lap when she first told me of the wedding. She talked of it again when Yrsa was born. She said she saw fire around Yrsa, that she was a fire child—Alys, what's the matter?"

Mother comes instantly to my side as I double over on the floor with the worst pain of my life, an awful burning in my head, as if I had received a great blow. The pain passes quickly, and I slump onto her knee.

"Alys? What happened?"

"I don't know . . . terrible pain. It's gone now."

Another commotion. Yrsa rushes back, obviously upset. Father looks into the shelter too.

"Mother! Jered needs us."

Something happened to his wife. That is what I felt. "Where is he?"

"Near the spirit chamber. I can find him. Mother, I'm afraid. Please. Now."

Father understands, as always. "Alys, go. Leave the drawings. The two of us will explain everything to the group if you're not back."

YRSA LEADS ME through the sleeping chamber into the spirit chamber and from there into a side passage near the west end. Jered is kneeling beside his wife, who is covered with blood. What happened is obvious. The broken rope lies to the side, in many coils and loops. Yrsa stands horrified, hand over mouth.

"Yrsa, bring water. Use the hide bag from the spirit chamber, near the hearth." Yrsa takes a torch and hurries away while I kneel to look at Alys. She is unconscious. Her hood lies beside her, broken. She has many cuts, and one leg is twisted. Jered has healing supplies and is swabbing a cut. He has already treated a big cut on the side of her head, where he had to cut a little of her hair away. He is distraught.

Above us is a huge black emptiness. Was she descending through it when she fell? Jered looks at me, and I point upward as a question. He shakes his head. We don't share language. How can he explain?

Yrsa returns with water. We hang the bag over a cave formation, and Jered repeatedly dips a cloth and strokes Alys, cleaning blood away from her face and arms. He has finished treating most of her cuts.

"Thank you, Yrsa. I think she will be all right. Now stay with her while I take Jered to Mother's map." I touch him, and he looks up. He understands what I want when I stand and beckon. Yrsa sits beside Alys and takes over Jered's mopping task.

JERED'S LIGHT makes the map's details stand out. I put my finger where Alys lies and trace a line straight upward, while I look a question at him. He understands and puts his finger on the upper entrance.

Jered and I are so closely connected that we don't need words. She lies directly below the upper entrance! She was descending from it when she fell!

I point toward the main entrance. Jered shakes his head, and I understand him. He means he has no choice but to use the upper entrance. I don't know why. Perhaps the main entrance too will be closed in the future, like the Riverside Cave. I will have to show him the long passage to the upper entrance, which is not on the map; Mother found it after the map was complete.

Starting with the upper entrance, I trace the path down to the spirit chamber with my finger. The route passes beyond the border Mother painted at the top of the map, goes almost to the western entrance, and doubles back to the big western chamber.

Jered understands, and his face floods with relief. He obviously thought he and Alys were trapped in the cave.

I take the time to lead him to the beginning of the passage. He nods and knows what he must do.

WE RETURN TO FIND ALYS STIRRING, writhing in an uncomfortable and painful sleep. Yrsa is relieved to see us.

"Yrsa, Jered must go to the upper entrance for help. One of us will need to stay with Alys."

Yrsa understands immediately. "I will care for her. I feel I know her, because she is like you."

Yrsa shows the broken end of the rope to me and Jered. The rope is made of many strands. Some have torn. The others have been cut.

Jered nods grimly. He had already discovered the truth.

Who would cut a climbing rope?

Alys mutters incoherently. Yrsa takes her hand and strokes it, gentle as a kitten, and Alys relaxes into more peaceful sleep. She is in good hands, and I leave to help explain to our group why they must stop whatever they are doing and turn their energy to building a fortress wall on the Riverside.

ALICE AND YRSA! Thank God. I don't wonder how they knew, or whether we are in the ancient time or the modern one, or anything else practical. I am simply relieved to see them. Yrsa leaves and quickly returns with water, which I badly need to clean Alys up. She is half-awake and suffering. I have given her liquid ibuprofen. I have a narcotic Tylenol, but I fear to use it when she's still recovering from shock.

Alice is agitated, and in a flash I know she has seen the paintings in the lower cave. Our eyes meet, and I sense her gratitude and concern. She knows of the impending attack and of the need for that big fortress wall.

I'm no longer surprised by what passes between us.

Alice must also see my fear of being trapped. She insistently leads me to the living chamber and her mother's cave map. With her finger, she traces a different route to the upper entrance—much longer, but one I can do on foot.

More relief. If only I were sure Alys would recover.

ALICE LEADS ME back to the bottom of the pit. She says a few words to Yrsa and then leaves. I understand; she has a great deal to tell her people. Yrsa remains, and I am touched that Alice trusts me enough to leave her daughter here.

Yrsa takes the hide bag and goes for more water. I am stroking Alys's face when she says, very quietly, "I'm sorry, Jarrett. I've gotten us in over our heads."

I nearly sob with relief.

"I'm glad you're awake. Yrsa is here. She and Alice sensed you were hurt."

"How will we ever get out of here?"

"Alice showed me a long route to the upper entrance."

"So we're not going to starve in the cave? That's good."

"How's your pain? I have narcotics if you need them."

She doesn't answer. She's out again.

YRSA IS GONE LONGER THAN I EXPECTED. When she reappears, in addition to the water bag she has a pottery bowl half full of large dark green leaves. She sets it beside Alys and looks up. "Let me tend her leg. The leaves will stop the pain. Can you cut her clothes away from the knee?"

Did she actually speak?

"Yrsa, can you understand me?"

She looks up and smiles when I say her name, but she has no idea what I said. I'm puzzled. Did I interpret her thoughts?

I gently straighten Alys's leg and cut the suit away from her swollen knee. Yrsa adds a little water to the bowl and crushes the leaves with her fingers. She packs Alys's knee with wet leaf mush and wraps it in hide, which she holds with one hand while with the other she fumbles for a long sinew cord. I whip out my adhesive roll and tape the hide. Yrsa is delighted. I tear off a short piece of tape and give it to her.

It isn't five minutes before Alys's moaning and squirming stop.

THE ROUTE TO THE UPPER ENTRANCE is easy but long, and the walk gives me time to think. I must contact Roger and Mira. I hope I can make a satellite call without encountering the stalker.

Reaching the top of Alys's Deep takes me every bit of three hours. Bringing a Stokes basket this way will be no problem—the entire route is wide and walking height.

I approach the upper entrance nervously; the stalker could be anywhere. I'll have to step onto the ledge to make the call, and I cautiously put my head out into the midnight twilight. Our rappel rope is still here. He has used it at least once and could again, but no one is in sight.

I step through the entrance onto the ledge, hoping I'm not being watched.

I PAY A YEARLY FORTUNE for satellite service but use it so rarely that I sometimes question its value. Not today. My heart pounds as I extract the phone from my pack and turn it on. Satellite service is iffy in the mountains. What will I do if the call fails?

The phone takes its time before it shows adequate connectivity.

Roger's phone goes to message. I try Mira, thinking *please.*

"Mira Kramnick."

"It's Jarrett, Mira. We're in trouble. Can you hear me?"

"Yes. Go on."

"Alys is hurt. We'll need to do a rescue up a route that is easy but hours long, or else sway her up a 300-foot pit, which would be quicker but scary. Your schedule hasn't changed? You're leaving Friday?"

"Yes, early. It's late afternoon Thursday here. Roger is out shopping. How did she get hurt? Will she be OK?"

"I hope so. She fell. Did I tell you she has been harassed by a stalker?"

"No."

"We rappelled down to the upper entrance Wednesday morning and descended the big pit she showed us. We rigged it with a single rope, but it has two pitches, with a ledge maybe a hundred feet above the bottom. We've been on that ledge several times today, because it also leads to a new area of the cave. Late in the day we returned to the ledge from the new area, and Alys was rappelling to the bottom when she fell. The rope had been cut, almost clear through."

Mean-sounding Polish expletive from the phone. "Of course you can't use official emergency services, because you shouldn't be there in the first place."

"I would, if it were absolutely essential. But you'll be here in two days, and I think she'll be OK that long. She has a broken leg, cuts and bruises, concussion. She was unconscious for a while, but she spoke to me before I climbed out to call you."

"You left her alone?"

"Alice and her daughter are taking care of her."

"Her daughter?"

"I'll explain later. Mira, you mustn't trust the downrope to the upper entrance. He could have cut that too. Bring plenty of rope. The pit needs 350 feet. You'll need 75 feet for the upper entrance. Bring a ton of rigging. And be watchful. That guy might still be around."

"Hi, Jarrett. Sorry to hear Alys is hurt." Roger has arrived, and my call is on speaker.

"How much did you hear?"

"Enough. We'll do our best. Good luck. God, we'll have to ship all that stuff too. And we were congratulating ourselves for being ready ahead of time. We have twelve hours until flight time. We can do it, but we'll have to hustle."

"Safe travel. One thing more. Please call Joel Harte. He bumbled into my place while Alys and I were preparing, and he knows our plans. He is in Europe this week anyway and may come to the cave. It would be like him. Tell him what's going on and warn him about the stalker."

Mira and Roger and I are all rescue-trained, but I have never done much real rescue work. They are active in the local cave rescue organization and have a ton of experience plus all the equipment.

I return by the long route. I could have brought rope to re-rig the pit, but that rope too would be vulnerable to sabotage. The round trip takes six hours.

I REACH ALYS at three in the morning to find her asleep under a heavy leather blanket. I stoop to check her pulse and respiration.

"You're back," she says quietly.

"How's your pain?"

"Not great. I would take Tylenol codeine."

"Can you sit up to swallow?"

"I could prop myself up on my right hip, but even that would hurt."

I dig out the tablet and a water bottle. She winces as I reach under her shoulders and lift her to drink. "Jarrett, don't look so damn worried. I'll recover."

"I was thinking about the next forty-eight hours while we wait for Roger and Mira."

Long silence. Then, "I learned a lot from Yrsa."

Another long pause, and I realize she has gone back to sleep.

I HAVE NEVER SPENT A LONGER WEEKEND.

Alys drifts in and out of consciousness, but she's awake more now than at first. "Yrsa has taught me a great deal, Jarrett. I hope I can remember the details later. I'm not talking about dreams. I'm living in a weird space."

"You told me about Yrsa when I returned from the upper entrance."

"I don't remember much from that first day, but I remember what Yrsa said. She calls this place the Benchland. The founders came here because they were tired of crowded village life, but now it's crowded here, which explains the houses down below—the Riverside, she calls that place. Yrsa knows her lineage. She is the granddaughter of one of the founding pairs and the great-granddaughter of the other. Her mother and grandmother and more women before them have been healers. Holy women, the leaders of their communities. Alice's mother is the village's leading figure. Alice will inherit that responsibility, and Yrsa after. She knows all that, and she's only nine. She knows far more about her own culture than a modern nine-year-old. She truly worships the spirit and feels part of it. There's more, but I'm tired."

"Could she understand you?"

"No, but she knows I understand her. I don't think she actually spoke. The incredibility of that escapes her. To her the spirit does many things we can't understand. It has no limits. I met her once by the pool in the spirit chamber. I haven't moved, but I was there. Can I have another sip of that water?"

She lies back, exhausted. "Yrsa spends time with me, checking on me. Comes to me at will, in our modern time. She says she and her mother can follow you and me anywhere, because the spirit joined us in the place she calls Hargard. Now I'm *really* tired."

Alys sleeps again, leaving me time to think about how much she has become part of my life.

YRSA VISITS MANY TIMES during our wait. She is as sunny as she is exceptional, but I don't hear her speak as I thought I did earlier. She is kind and gentle with Alys. She approves of modern bandages and has learned how to apply them.

Alys has learned from Yrsa that an effort is already underway to build the fortress wall and prepare to fight. Alice's father is in charge, and her uncle is leading the construction. Almost a hundred people spend every moment making arrows and cutting trees, in a defensive mobilization with the intensity of the Manhattan Project. All based on paintings Alice will make afterward.

The upper entrance will play an important role in the defense scheme. Alice and her mother have been scouting lookout posts. A sentry will be posted on the ledge outside the entrance, which has a good view of the shelf and of the river for some distance in both directions. Another will watch from the mountaintop, which overlooks the river northward for many miles and southeastward nearly to the sea. Perhaps on one of her trips to the upper entrance, Alice will see Mira and sketch her.

I'M RELIEVED when I hear Roger and Mira working on rigging at the top of the pit. I catch their attention by shouting. We can't understand each other; the pit makes every sound into a symphony of echoes.

The situation improves when Roger lowers a walkie-talkie. "Jarrett, can you hear me?"

"Hey. I'm glad you guys are here. You're both OK?"

"Exhausted," Mira says. "How's Alys?"

"She's awake about a third of the time, although that's improving. Broken leg still broken. Cuts are mending. Several will need stitches."

"She's right below us? Can we lower the gear safely?"

"She's on a foam mattress, and I've towed her out of the way."

Roger says, "You said the ledge was on the west side? I'm rigged on the east side, to drop gear."

"That should work."

"First load coming down. Duffel bag. Two more to follow. Then Mira, and she can help you with the basket, which I'll lower last."

"Did you meet the stalker?"

"Yes. He's under control. We'll tell you all about it."

Under control? What could that mean? None of this disturbs Alys's sleep.

"Here comes your duffel bag. I'll take it off rope."

"Another coming now, on another rope. I'll take the first rope back."

Half an hour later we all sit beside Alys, who sleeps through the entire procedure. We unpack the gear and then rest and talk.

I can see Roger and Mira are tired. "Are you guys ready to do the carry, or do you want to sleep the night here first?"

"I think now," Mira says. "It won't be a bit easier tomorrow."

"Tell me about your encounter with the stalker."

Mira rolls her eyes, leaving Roger to answer. "I have a journal going. I'll add an entry later and you can read the whole story. Bottom line is he's shackled securely into his Jeep. And he's completely nuts."

THE THREE OF US lay out the Stokes basket and lift Alys into it by using the foam mattress as a sling. She groans and opens her eyes.

"Mira. Roger. What day is it?"

"Saturday night," Roger says. "Actually early Sunday morning. If your schedule permits, Jarrett and I will carry you up to the car."

Mira is surprised. "What am *I* supposed to do?"

"The carry will take hours," I say. "To sway the basket up to the mountaintop, we'll need a second rope down from the cliff. You can have that ready long before we need it."

"I'm a patient person," Alys says, and perhaps she even tries a smile. "Where's the stalker?"

"Mira punched him out, and we shackled him into his Jeep. He won't be going anywhere."

Alys lifts a corner of the heavy leather blanket she has been sleeping under for two days. "What are we going to do with this? It's a brand-new ancient artifact. From Alice and her daughter. We have a great deal to tell you about them."

Mira raises her eyebrows. "Like the wooden toy you found. We'll have to take it with us. I don't even want to *hear* how you got it."

I gather up all our things and load our packs and gear bags. Alys's pack and our two big bags will stay here for now; we'll make a final trip down for them. Mira straps on her harness and ascenders and starts up the rope. I look back at the place that's been home since Alys was hurt, and then Roger and I begin the long carry. Alys is asleep again.

NEARLY A WEEK PASSES before I see Roger's journal. Here it is, without comment.

> *7/9 - We'll fly on Friday the 13th? No wonder we got seats on moment's notice. Jarrett sent email about a dream in which cavers entering the upper*

entrance face some threat. Alys had a similar dream. My rational mind says coincidence, but alarms sound in the part of me that knows Alice's Cave.

7/12 - Jarrett calls on the satellite link. Alys is injured. The dream threat was no coincidence. She's at the bottom of a 300-foot pit. We're ready to leave tomorrow morning, but now we need to add rescue gear—Stokes basket, medical kit, extra rope and rigging. Assembling that stuff takes until midnight. Jarrett wants us to talk to Joel Harte. We leave a long message on his voicemail.

7/13 - Painfully long flight gives me time to think about all the caving trips I've made with Jarrett, starting in high school. From the first until now, every single one has been a circus. I never know what will happen, but it's always something. On this trip the chaos comes from a psycho. Alys fell because her rope was cut by a guy who has been stalking her for years. Mira and I might encounter him when we get to the cave. How do I get into things like this?

When Mira and I first saw Jarrett with Alys, bright and pretty, and a high achiever, we thought they might be converging into a relationship. Jarrett said not, but still.

7/14 - Land in Stockholm, rent a car. I slept on the plane; Mira naps while I drive. Roadwork stops us for two hours. While we wait, we reach Joel Harte. He's in Stockholm, in the airport. Plans to come to the cave tomorrow. We tell him everything. Warn him he might meet Alys's stalker.

We stop briefly in Rivermouth about five PM and turn onto the difficult road after eight. At about ten, we leave the car on the road and hike to the mountaintop, arriving not long before midnight, still twilight. We see Jarrett's car in the trees, tarped as usual. The bad guy's Jeep is not far away. We spot him shortly after, lying at the cliff edge, looking down Jarrett's rope. Two days ago this nut case descended to the upper entrance and went to the big pit, where he found and sabotaged the rappel rope. By now he probably knows that rope is gone. What is he looking for?

Mira sneaks up on him. She comes to within a few feet—she can walk as quietly as a cat—and says, "Freeze." He goes nuts—jumps backward with a shriek, grabs a substantial rock, and charges Mira. You poor man, you picked the wrong person. Mira is five two and weighs about a hundred and ten, but she's rock-hard and grew up on the back streets of Krakow, the first person in her family not to earn a living as a menial or a criminal. She stands calmly as he rushes her. When he draws back to hit her with the rock, she strikes like a snake and he goes down, lights out. We drag him to his Jeep and improvise handcuffs out of shackles and steel cable tie. He wakes up in the back seat. We leave him two water bottles but have no time for sympathy. We do take a cell phone picture of him cuffed into his Jeep.

I hike back to the car and park it on the mountaintop, violating rental company rules. We rig a new downrope to the upper entrance. Before we descend, we check on our prisoner. He rants insanely. He's pretty crazy.

SATURDAY 14 JULY

Two days since I cut the rope. I felt something dreadful down the deep hole then. Yesterday I went back in there to check on the rope. Gone! It broke! I hope it was she who fell, but it makes no difference. No one will be climbing out of that hole.

Then it came for me. I couldn't bear facing it in the dark, and I bolted for the entrance. I felt it behind me as I ran. I felt it until I was in the daylight outside. It is an ancient creature of the dark.

Not knowing what happened when the rope broke is awful. I can't go into the cave again, because that thing will have me. I lie at the cliff watching the entrance below. I can still feel the horror down there.

SUNDAY 15 JULY

I squeeze my eyes closed and try to blot what happened from my memory. I was attacked by a madwoman. A psychotic. She crept up behind me and tried to terrify me into jumping over the edge. When I attacked her, she shot me with some new kind of techno-weapon and knocked me out. I woke up an hour ago when she and a man were locking me into my jeep. My wrists are crossed in front of me, tied together with shackles. I can move them around a bit, but not far.

They too must die.

I try to think. Four are in the cave now. The man and the madwoman went down the cliff. They must return sometime. My gun is in the glove box, out of reach. If I had it I could make them release me.

I can move my legs and feet as I sit in the open Jeep door. How can I use my feet to get the gun?

A twisty three-foot branch lies nearby on the ground. By turning half over I can reach it with the toe of my boot. I try to pull it toward me, but it only moves farther away. I reposition myself and try again. And fail again. And again. I rest and try once more, with a different angle. No use.

I draw my boot up to me, loosen the laces, and kick the boot and sock off. I try reaching for the stick with my bare toes.

Ants sting my foot, but I don't give up.

I am exhausted, but my spirits are higher, because the sun is coming up. And I have the stick.

I CAN BARELY REACH the glove box lock with the stick. I poke and prod, but nothing happens. I shift my position and try again. I must not give up. Eventually the glove box falls open. The papers slide out. The pistol and my water pump pliers fall out and land on the front seat floor.

Out of reach.

I turn my body sideways with the stick between my feet and reach for the pistol. I can touch it but not move it. I hook the trigger guard with a projecting twig and pull. The gun slides to the door and falls onto the ground. I can reach it with the stick. In five minutes I have it. I can't reach the pliers. If I had them I could remove the shackle bolts.

I blow dirt off the gun and check the clip, which is full. I twist myself back as they left me, slumped against the seat, turned so they can't see the gun. I wait.

I feel the horror from the deep hole, sniffing for me at the cliff. I must stay calm.

WHEN THE PSYCHOTIC WOMAN appears at the cliff edge, I scream for help. She looks, detaches herself from the rope, and comes toward me.

She does not realize I have the pistol until I aim it at her chest.

"Release me." The cave thing is at the cliff edge. It followed her up the rope. I can barely control my terror.

She hesitates.

I point the pistol above her shoulder and fire a shot. "Release me or I will kill you." My hands shake.

"I will need to detach the shackle behind you. Roll over."

Her accent! I thought so before, but now I'm sure. Russian! She is behind all my torture for so many years!

"No. Take the bolt out of the front shackle. Use the pliers on the front seat floor."

She hesitates.

"Do it now or I will shoot you."

I hold the pistol almost against her chest as she opens the shackle. The cables fall away and I am free. But the cave horror is nearer.

I HAVE VERY LITTLE TIME. "Turn around and put your hands behind you. Give me your car keys."

"I don't have the car keys. They're in the cave with my husband."

Her car is close to the cliff. I shackle her wrists to the front bumper. I will use my car to push hers off the cliff. She will go with it, and my years of harassment will end.

I go to the cliff and cut the rope. Her husband won't be coming up at all. No one will be coming up.

It is torture to stand near the cliff. I made a terrible mistake by going there. Now the monster knows where I am. When I start my Jeep, I can hardly think for heart-pounding shaking terror, because it is here on the hilltop.

I line up the Jeep behind her car. I am shaking so hard that I can barely control my hands. It knows! It knows I cut the rope. It knows I intend to kill her.

It cannot stop me. Nothing can stop me.

WHAT NOW? A man running toward me—from below, not from the cave. Almost upon me. He has a weapon!

I snatch the gun from the seat, but the thing from the cave is too close, coming from the other side. I cannot stay here. I throw the car into reverse and back away fast. The man follows, but he is slow. I slip the car into drive and spin the wheel, turning away from hilltop and cave. But the creature is in front of the Jeep! I can feel it. It will kill me. I swerve away. Speed and distance are my only hope.

It comes closer, still in front of me.

Upon me!

I spin the wheel again and floor the accelerator.

THE STOKES BASKET is a heavy, awkward carry. We are four hours into the trip to the upper entrance, and Roger and I are dog tired.

Alys is mostly conscious. How could she not be, with all that jolting? "Jarrett, I'm finally fully awake. I've been wondering. Did he cut the rope?"

"Looks that way."

"If he's that crazy, he could do something to Mira."

I've been concerned about that, and I'm sure Roger has been thinking about it too. We're near the top, and we press on without answering.

"Here they come!" Mira's voice is a relief. Who is she talking to? Seconds later, I see her—with Joel. They are barely inside the entrance.

Roger and I set the basket down, and Mira runs to him. "I am *so* glad to see you. Weird stuff happens here. We owe Joel a lot of thanks. He arrived at the critical moment." She looks down at Alys. "You're awake! Are you doing OK?"

"I've been better." But she smiles. "That sun out on the ledge looks good."

"We need to rig another rope before we can sway the basket up the hill," Mira says. "Too busy staying alive to attend to that."

Roger and I carry the basket out onto the ledge, and Alys sighs with pleasure in the sun. We break out food and water and sit to hear what happened.

"I PARKED ON THE ROAD," Joel says, "and walked to the top of the hill. I wasn't completely unarmed—I had a tire iron. But when I was close to the top, I heard a gunshot."

"Our guy had a gun," Mira says. "We never checked for weapons. The shot was to convince me it was loaded."

Roger is shocked. "How did he get loose? He was tied in securely."

"He made me unlock him. He screamed for help and then held the gun on me. He shackled me to the bumper of our car and was going to push it off the cliff. Me with it. Nice guy."

Roger shudders and pulls Mira to him. "But crazy. When we tied him up he raved about government persecution. He thought we were agents."

"He was maneuvering his Jeep behind your car," Joel says. "I shouted and charged him with my tire iron. He picked up his gun and was turning toward me. Then he froze. He was terrified—big eyes, open mouth."

"I couldn't see any of that," Mira says.

"He jammed the Jeep into reverse and backed away toward the trees. Then he took off forward at a sprint, swerving back and forth as if dodging live fire. Insane driving. He headed south, down the ridge, still swerving. He must have been going eighty when he went off the cliff."

"Oh, God," Alys says. "Did he end up on the shelf?"

"He was much farther south than that. I think he went all the way to the river—600 feet down. I was too far away to see it, but I heard the explosion."

SILENCE.

"I'll never know who he was," Alys says.

Roger reaches into his pack for his phone. "We took a picture when we tied him into his Jeep." He turns the phone on, finds the picture, and hands the phone to Alys.

"Oh, my God. Bill Alberts. *Him?* I knew him in high school, in the caving club, in Virginia. *He* is the guy who has been stalking me for years? He seemed like a nice, quiet kid."

"He sure was nuts," Joel says. "And obviously badly frightened of something. I wonder what?"

"Are you kidding?" Mira shakes her head. "This cave is not an ordinary place. You know very well what he was afraid of. And with good reason."

AN HOUR LATER we are gathered at the top. I retrieve Kristin's car and begin setting up a bed for Alys, but she objects. "Jarrett, I have no intention of lying on my back all the way to Stockholm. We have things to discuss. Let's recline the passenger seat and slide it back. You're clever. Figure out a way to support my leg."

Roger and I make a final trip into the cave to retrieve the gear and Alys's pack. I descend and attach the loads one by one; Roger hauls. I start coiling the rope but he stops me. "Mira and I can use them."

We carry the gear to the ledge outside the entrance. This time I climb and haul, while Roger loads.

When the car is packed and Alys is settled to my satisfaction, Mira looks in through the open passenger-side window.

"Will we ever hear what happened in the cave?"

Alys smiles. "As soon as I'm out of the hospital. The bottom line is we came here for a purpose, and it was fulfilled. When will you arrive in Stockholm?"

"We'll sleep the night here. Probably all morning too. Then we'll spend a few days in the cave, because I also have a purpose."

Alice's sketch of Mira inside the upper entrance is part of the reason we're all here.

"Jarrett, will you hand me the small pouch out of the front pocket of my pack?" Alys finds a business card, writes on it, and hands it to Mira. "Please do me the favor of staying at my apartment. I have plenty of room. This code will get you into the garage and the door. I suspect I'll be there before you will. We have a great deal to talk about."

Joel turns to Mira and Roger. "I'd like to go into the cave with you. When you guys leave I'll follow you to Stockholm and go right to the airport. I have to be in London for a Thursday meeting."

"Joel," I say, "thank you. You saved us all."

"I didn't do it for you, you know. I did it for Alys."

JERED AND ALYS have left the cave, Yrsa says, but they will return. That relieves my concern, but I am too busy for anything now except helping Mother with the preparations for whatever lies ahead.

We can't train fighters and build the wall at the same time, because the same people do both—our twenty-nine men and older boys. They work hard all day bringing tree trunks to the Riverside. Uncle Druian is in charge of that work. He has already drawn a complete design for the wall, showing more detail than I remember from the paintings.

After the evening meal the men meet behind the growing wall and talk about the fighting. Some women will fight as well, the experienced hunters, including Mother. We will have nearly thirty-five fighters all told, some shooting from behind the wall, others standing back to fight enemies who manage to come beyond the wall or over it. We already have lookouts at the upper entrance and on top of the mountain. They will warn us of approaching enemies by dropping rocks onto the bench. We clear the area where the rocks will fall, and we always have an older child watching for that signal and keeping small children away. This is Father's idea.

If Aunt Inge were here she would fight alongside the men. Mother is of her kind.

THE MEN START BY CUTTING and hauling the three largest and tallest trunks, the ones that will stand at the ends and the middle of the wall to support all the others. Each is huge and heavy—more than three armspans long and almost three handspans across. The bullock and cart strain to carry them. When the cart can come no closer to the Riverside, men and bullock work together to drag the trunks the rest of the way.

As soon as the big trunks arrive, the men start digging the trench, using flint shovels with stout wooden handles. The trench is enormous—one full armspan deep and five long. Underground rocks make the digging slow and difficult. When that work is finally complete, the men stand the first of the big posts into place. All the men drag the thing into position, and then most of them go to the smaller end and lift as high as they can reach. They support the lifted end temporarily by propping it with shorter posts, and then some of them move toward the butt end, where they lift the trunk higher while standing on a sturdy scaffold we use for building houses. Eventually the butt end slides and tips into the hole. Two men stand on the scaffold and reach nearly to the top of the big post to hold it in place while the others pile large rocks around its base to hold it.

The first post! This feels like a victory, but we're all aware that we have taken more than a halfmonth and the wall is barely begun—and that placing the huge posts is dangerous. When the post slid, one man was knocked from the scaffold and hurt. We have two more big posts to place—with only twenty-eight men.

We need about forty smaller posts of different lengths. Father and Uncle Druian are always thinking about how to arrange gaps in the wall for arrow slits. Cutting the posts to length takes time. The finished ends must be cut off cleanly. Younger boys can do that job, which requires more patience than strength. They use long blades of glarestone, drawing them back and forth across the log. Each cut takes a half day. We have only five of those cutting blades, and they are in use all day, every day. The boys must be careful; the blades are fragile.

We start with the six posts that were to go into the new house, and every day the men cut one or two more and haul them in. By the end of the first month we have nearly enough posts to finish the wall. After that, half the men continue to cut posts, while the others turn to completing the wall, one section at a time. All the men are busy from morning until night. Uncle Druian is everywhere.

EARLY IN OUR BATTLE PREPARATIONS I dream of Aunt Inge. I tell her everything. I take her to the upper entrance with its view of the Riverside so she can appreciate the work we are doing. The dream seems real, and when I wake I wonder if it could be a message about the upper entrance. Yrsa and I visit Hargard in the afternoon, and I tell her of the dream. She remembers Aunt Inge and Uncle Sigurd well. We decide the dream is a summons, that we must visit the upper entrance.

The walk is long. We carry only water and torches. We pass the top of the deep pit where Alys fell. A rope hangs into the pit. Jered's rope. We used one like it when we descended into the Riverside Cave to see the paintings. We came from Hargard that time too, into Jered's time.

We are nervous and cautious. We know this part of the cave well, but it is not the same. Could I be bringing Yrsa into danger?

She is following my thoughts and looks at me. "It feels safe but is all changed."

We walk slowly downward toward the upper entrance. We stop when we hear a sound. My heart races. I peer around the last corner and see Aunt Inge. My dream has become real.

But not Aunt Inge. A woman very like her, with her appearance and size and obvious strength. But a different person. She is wearing clothes like Jered's. Her hood is off, sitting on the ground beside her. She is kneeling, coiling rope. Other coils of rope lie beside her.

She is Aunt Inge come back to life except for her hair, which is fine and golden like Aunt Inge's—but short. I am stunned. I have never seen a grown woman with short hair. Why would she cut it?

I was shocked when I first saw Jered without his beard. Now, a woman with short hair. Could that be normal in their world? I cannot imagine cutting my hair.

She steps outside the upper entrance, stands on the ledge, and shouts something upward. We cannot hear a reply. She returns to the cave, puts on her hood, straps something around her. Then she climbs the rope and disappears.

Yrsa and I look at each other, astonished.

THE CUTTING AND HAULING are finished at last, and the wall grows daily. Already half the posts are standing upright, and half of those are bound into place with hemp. We are congratulating ourselves at a high-spirited group meal on the Riverside—Uncle Druian and his hard-working men are drinking beer—when a runner appears on the path from the river and staggers into our midst. He is Einar, a Rivermouth boy. Soon afterward a second boy appears, Einar's younger brother Randi. Both are exhausted. They have run from Rivermouth in two days.

Einar and Randi's father sold Uncle Druian our bullock and cart. He sent the boys to give us news about raiders, the first known in Rivermouth for many years. We stand in a circle around the two boys, hearing what they came to tell us.

"They are coming down the coast toward Rivermouth. Several boats arriving from the north have seen them camped—a great horde of fighters. Far more than a hundred. The men in Rivermouth are planning to surprise them well north of the village and believe they can drive the raiders off. Our father thinks that if we succeed, the raiders will turn upriver and come here."

Father answers for us. "As you see, we are already preparing to fight raiders. But we didn't know they would bring so many or come so soon. You have done us a great service. Perhaps saved us."

"The Rivermouth men believe they might face the enemy five days from now," Einar says. "The raiders could be here three day after that."

Mother stands back and looks at the two boys. "You have done your job well, and we will always remember you in our telling of these times. Now you need rest. Please share our meal with us and stay with us tonight. We will give you food for your return."

CAN WE SURVIVE AN ATTACK by so many enemies? I discuss it with Mother, Father, and Uncle Druian. We have a safer alternative—to retreat to the Benchland and give up the Riverside, with its crops and animals.

Mother is confident. "We are warned, and we have a good plan. We won't face hundreds of men at once. They will have to come onto the Riverside single file. All the children will be safe on the Benchland, so a defeat would not ruin us forever."

"It is they who will be defeated," I say. "I know it, for I have seen the paintings I will make afterward. I suspected it before I saw the paintings, because Uncle Sigurd said we must prepare to defend the Riverside. Not abandon it."

Father stands. "I believe that too, Alys, but hard work lies before us. More attackers means we need more arrows."

I take great pride in my parents—our elders, now, and our leaders. They show no fear.

YRSA AND I VISIT HARGARD the next morning, at her insistence. We don't speak at first, but simply succumb to the mystery of the place where we were united with Jered and Alys. Their absence makes the room feel empty.

"They will return, and soon," Yrsa says.

"Eventually they will leave and not return."

"Mother! They will never leave. They will be here forever."

As we lurch down the terrible road to the river, Alys—reclining in the passenger seat with her splinted leg in front of her—suffers in silence. I drive at a creep, but the ride is still rough, and I'm relieved when we reach the smooth river road. I look over at her. "I'm glad that's behind us. Are you OK?"

"I'm fine, and we have many reasons to be glad. I'm recovering, and we escaped a madman."

"And we finally have time to talk. We need that."

"I spent some difficult hours. Not because I thought I was mortally injured, but because I thought we were trapped. I was aware of that possibility the moment I fell."

"You remember falling? What did you think?"

As she considers what to say, we slow down to pass a cluster of emergency vehicles at the edge of the road, a half mile south of the shelf. The burnt-out hulk of the

Jeep lies partly in the river, far below. We drive on, silently agreeing not to come forward with what we know.

Alys considers the river scenery in silence. I suspect she has forgotten my question.

"Jarrett, would you please stop the car?"

I pull off to the left. When I roll down the window, the car fills with the sound of the river. To our right, a ring of hills surrounds a substantial acreage of crops. "The government is making better use of the land than I did. Those fields are new."

"Isn't this where the wall was built? The Riverside?"

The river has changed its course, and erosion has changed the shape of the land, but the hills are unmistakably the same ones Alice painted. I am struck by a thought. "Do you suppose we could find remnants of that mighty wall?"

Alys laughs. "We can try, but not this trip. Look at me."

I drive on. Later, she says, "What did I think on the way down? Deep regret. I didn't think I would live through the fall. I hadn't had time to process what happened to us with Alice and Yrsa, and I didn't want to die without understanding that miracle."

Five minutes later I realize she is asleep, and she dozes on and off all the way to Stockholm. Once she is safe in the hospital Sunday evening, I retreat exhausted to her apartment and sleep twelve hours solid, too tired for dreams.

ALYS SPENDS THREE NIGHTS in the hospital, until the neurologist is convinced she has no permanent damage from the concussion. I spend much of that time with her. The nurses kindly offer me food trays, which I accept, and a cot, which I decline. Alys's apartment, even empty, is a better choice for sleeping than a hospital.

All that time alone, and still we don't talk through what happened. We both avoid it. Still processing.

Alys emerges Wednesday morning with many stitches and a cast that comes above the knee. She will be using crutches until the cast comes off. I drive her home in Kristin's car; fortunately, we can keep it another few days.

The apartment is no longer empty. Roger and Mira greet us at the door, fully recovered from their time of too much craziness and too little sleep. "We left the cave yesterday afternoon," Mira says, "and stayed in a hotel last night. Joel left when we did. He flies out this evening." She turns to me. "We fly Friday night. What are your plans?"

"They begin with food and a long talk. Alys, are you up to having dinner in a restaurant?"

"Absolutely not. I look like a train-wreck victim. But after a week of cave snacks and hospital food, I'm ready for a real meal. We can have dinner brought here from our choice of local restaurants. Let's not talk of anything serious until we've had enough to eat."

"I HARDLY KNOW WHERE TO START." Alys is kicked back in her living room after a glass of wine and a good meal. Her cast rests on a footstool. "Mira, the map you sent us is at the center of what happened. We used that connection to get to the lower cave. Did you go there?"

"No. After we saw the spirit chamber and the living chamber, we returned to the ledge in the middle of the pit and went to the new area you found—the small spirit room. Then we took Joel to see the ancient western entrance. We cut the visit short because we were concerned about you."

"I'm sorry you didn't go to the lower cave. It's a big part of the story. The exit is closed by breakdown now."

"Like the western entrance," Roger says.

I shake my head. "Not like it at all. Alice's people abandoned the western entrance early on and moved east to the living chamber and the shelf. They never lived at the western entrance again. So it doesn't have paintings."

Mira snaps to attention. "Tell me more."

"At the end of the lower cave, before the closure, are huge wall paintings of a major battle. I photographed them, of course."

I bring up the images on my laptop.

"Where *is* this place?" Mira has her nose to the laptop screen.

"They called it the Riverside. Downstream from the shelf nearly a mile. See the cave entrance? That's the lower cave as it was then."

"That's some wall." Roger's turn to glue himself to the laptop.

"After Alice saw the paintings, the entire community devoted every moment to building it."

Mira's eyebrows go up. "Alice *saw* them? They look like her paintings."

Alys pours wine all around. "They are. You'll understand in a bit."

"How did they haul those enormous trunks?" Roger is looking at details, and I bring up the smaller painting, showing an oxcart and ten men hauling a tree trunk.

"Wheels! They had wheels!" Mira is as excited as I expected. "So Alice saw a picture of the wall before it was built? Like when you showed her a tablet before she painted it?"

"That was in a dream. This time she actually went to the closed tunnel and saw paintings she would make later."

"How?"

Alys glances at me. "That brings us to the main story. Jarrett and I shared a profound spiritual experience with Alice and Yrsa, her nine-year-old daughter. It happened in the small spirit room, which adjoins the spirit chamber."

Mira nods. "It has that same presence. How did Alice and her daughter get there?"

"They swam. Yrsa discovered the connection when she was very young. She believes the room is the home of the spirit and goes there often."

Alys sips her wine. "I don't know how long the four of us were together there. I lost track of time. We became a single being in a ring of fire. Everything I believed about the universe collapsed. It was Yrsa who led us to this epiphany. A little girl."

Silence.

"All four of us were physically together in that room," I say. "I think we were in both times at once. Yrsa understood they should visit the lower cave immediately. When they did, they found the exit closed and saw the paintings as they are today"

Another long silence follows. "I don't even know how Jarrett feels about what happened," Alys says. "I fell shortly afterward, and we've put off talking about it."

The wine has put me in an expansive mood. "You should *see* how much those two look alike. Alice and Alys. Twins. And Alice felt the pain when Alys fell."

Alys's turn to be surprised. "How do you know *that*?"

"I understood it from Yrsa. After our time in Hargard I mostly understood her, although I don't think she actually spoke."

"Hargard?" This from Roger.

"That's what Yrsa calls the spirit room," Alys says. "She waited with me while Jarrett climbed the long route to the upper entrance. I was in a strange mental state, drifting in and out. Yrsa told me many things. I know her well."

"And?" Mira is a scientist first. "What does all this mean?"

"Mira, I told you. Jarrett and I have not talked about what it means. But we are not what we were, either of us. It's a new world."

"WHAT'S NEXT?" Practical issues are Roger's bailiwick.

Mira stands. "Roger Kramnick, I must see those paintings."

Roger sighs. "I have to leave Friday night, as scheduled. I'm going to San Francisco next week, remember? I fly out Monday."

"I need more cave time too," Alys says. "Why don't you come back when I'm healed, and we'll go to the cave together? My cast comes off in the middle of September. A good-weather trip of a few days is plausible then. You might have to help me up the rope."

"We're a self-funded rescue organization," Roger says quickly. "Taking Mira to the cave now makes more dollar sense. Rifleshot trip. See the paintings and get out. Fourteen hours driving and eight caving. Twenty-two-hour project, and we have more than forty-eight to do it."

Alys meets my eyes, and my world shifts out of its orbit. The memory of our bonding with Alice and Yrsa pulls me into a kind of flashback, once again awash in emotion. Fire springs up around us, and I know who I am.

The memory fades, and Alys's living room comes back into focus as we emerge from another universe. How long have we been gone? Roger and Mira seem puzzled.

That experience ends it for our old separate selves. Our ambiguous relationship disintegrates, leaving a bone-deep mutual understanding that the two of us belong together. Have always been together. The words we have cautiously left unsaid won't be needed now.

Alys breaks the silence. "We'll fly the two of you here in the middle of September."

Mira's eyebrows go up again.

I look around at all of them. "We'll need witnesses."

YRSA AND I will have to watch the battle from a distance—from the upper entrance. I want to stay on the Riverside, but Mother will not hear of it, even though she will be there with Father. "If Olaf should be lost, I would want to fight alongside him to the end. You and Yrsa are a different story. Our future depends on you."

"Mother, the paintings! I know from the spirit that Yrsa and I will be safe."

"What would you say to Yrsa and her own little girl, a few years from now? You must decide where Yrsa should be and then stay there with her."

FATHER THINKS THE RAIDERS WILL SEND SCOUTS, and when they do not return, the large group will attack out of vengeance. But the raider scouts remain at a distance. Eight days after the Rivermouth boys leave, the lookout sees a few men on the mountain south of us, with its view of the entire Riverside. They surely see our wall, but from above. Father thinks they might not realize how tall it is.

The wall is not finished; the last two posts have not been cut to length and placed. Dozens of hemp fastenings are not yet tied. When we learn of the scouts, we abandon the posts and everyone ties hemp fastenings.

Yrsa and I leave in midevening to begin the trek to the upper entrance. The children and most of the women are already gathered on the Benchland. Only the fighting group remains on the Riverside.

We don't arrive at the upper entrance until nearly midnight. We are both tired, but the sight of raider campfires along the river makes us anxious.

"They could attack tonight," Yrsa says, fretting.

"Yrsa, the paintings show an early-morning battle. And if the raiders intended to attack tonight, they wouldn't build campfires." Despite my reassurance, neither of us sleeps much, and each time we wake, the raider encampment is bigger.

THEY SWARM THE RIVERSIDE early in the morning in a large group, running hard. When they reach the wall they pile up in confusion, and Mother later says that throughout the attack, disorganization slowed the raiders down. Instead of fifteen or twenty enemies at any time outside the wall, Father's men fight ten. We have sixteen fighters at the wall. Mother takes her place there some of the time.

The raiders scream and throw flaming brands onto the wall, but the trunks are green, and the wall never catches fire. The enemies try to swarm over the rocky ridge behind the upstream end of the wall, but the slope is steep, and once at the top they face four or five of our men. The raiders try shooting through the wall's arrow slits with slightly more success; my cousin Valdrik, Uncle Druian's youngest son, is struck in the leg.

Before the morning is half gone, the attackers give up the fight and flee upriver. A few of their injured join them, but the bodies of more than half their number lie in a bloody jumble below the path, a horrific sight.

We lose no one. Valdrik's injury is serious, but after treating it Mother says he will recover.

Yrsa and I see the entire battle from above, and when it ends we return to the Riverside to help clean up. Our battle-weary men carry the raider bodies to the river on the bullock cart—this requires five trips—and set them afloat, an end more honorable than they deserve, but Mother and I and Yrsa all agree the dead should not remain near us.

We find no enemies alive. Our men return with some raider weapons—bows, arrows, long knives, shields—but many fallen raiders had been stripped of weapons by their fleeing comrades. We retrieve no redmetal blades or points, and the flint arrowheads and knives are crude next to our own.

Yrsa and I will visit Hargard this afternoon, out of gratitude for the wisdom of the spirit. This evening, with all the others, we will gather on the Benchland to celebrate our victory, and tomorrow will be a day of rest for the men and boys whose hard work saved us. Today is the equinox, and from now on the equinox will always remind us of the battle for the Riverside.

WHEN I FIRST MET ALICE in the spirit chamber, I feared I was losing the ability to know what was real. Finding the tablets she made reassured me, and living with her two paintings of me reminds me daily that the world is beyond my comprehending. I have gradually come around to Alice and Yrsa's point of view—nothing is impossible, and no explanations are needed. I no longer beat my head against the wall trying to understand the things that happened in Alice's Cave. I simply accept them—even Yrsa speaking to me when Alys lay injured and Alice seeing paintings she hadn't yet made. This makes it easier to accept the everyday incomprehensible miracles, such as conception and birth, and the hints of the infinite that are part of loving.

The ancient people saw the transcendent as the work of the spirit of their cave. I see it as the manifestation of a spirit we share with everyone and everything. Not so different, those views.

THE AUTUMNAL EQUINOX brings us back to Hargard at last, for our fifth anniversary. We never intended to wait so long. Last year I was recovering from a caving injury. Two years in a row it was early winter that made the trip impossible—before that, the birth of our daughter.

The others aren't here. Roger and Mira are busy, although we saw them before we left Baltimore. Kristin and Joanie are in the US for the fall trip through the national parks they've promised themselves since they met. Joel sent his best wishes.

A fire would be an affront to the cave, so we wear jackets and depend on an LED lamp, a dim orange. Alys leans back against me with her arm around the little girl sitting in front of us, who is four today. She is excited to be in this place, because we've told her it is truly magical and is responsible for her very being. She has dreamed of it regularly all her life. Once again I am struck by how much she looks like her mother—and like Alice and her own daughter, who have been on my mind. Of course I hope to see them.

This chamber blurs the distinction between then and now, reality and dream. When we were married here, Alice and Yrsa—they came from their battle triumph—were real to Kristin, enough so to spur her crisis of faith and departure from the church. And what of the fire that rose around us, and the joining of spirit? Real enough to unite Alys and me, more than the words Kristin spoke. The richness of my life grew from what occurred here.

Still, my mind wants to simplify, wants place and time to be singular and well defined. It would prefer to wall off what it can't understand and call it Dream, or perhaps Miracle of God.

A small hand on my arm brings me back to Hargard and my family. Yrsa looks up at me, the light catching her blue eyes. "Daddy, look! Other people!"

She does not question what she sees.

The Benchland Saga
Timeline of principal ancient characters and events

year

Warriors Bk 3		0	Elvdal raid
			Fosser raid
		5	Fire wedding
Rockslide Bk 1		10	Benchland discovered
		15	Ana born
		20	
		25	
Light from the Stream Bk 2			Ana and Olaf marry
		30	Alys born
		35	
		40	
Inheritance Bk 2			
		45	Alys and Kyle marry
Warriors Epilogue Bk 3			Yrsa born
		50	
Rockslide Epilogue Bk 1			
		55	
Child of Fire Bk 3			Battle of the Riverside
		60	

Acknowledgments

WE BEGAN WRITING *ROCKSLIDE* IN 2011, and nearly five years later we are still debating a few words in *Ring of Fire*. The Benchland series has been a long-term writer's workshop for us—and a challenge, in which we have struggled to learn about life, culture, and technology in the late Neolithic.

We've had help from many people throughout this project, and a great deal of help with *Ring of Fire*.

Our month-long beta reading event brought many readers and several hundred comments, and we appreciate every one. This was our fourth reading event, and our readers have become quite discerning. Their observations brought about an astonishing number of changes to the text. Our readers are our most valuable critics, our editors, and our consciences. Our teachers.

Thanks to Willow Bunu, Yvonne Fairbairn, Eric Hosler, and Nicholas G. Williams, for comments that significantly improved the text. Joyce Gibson Roach's observations resulted in major changes to *Warriors*. We are grateful to Frances J. Sawaya for her professional help and keen storytelling insight; she too brought about significant changes. Louis Jaeckel found the majority of the book's hard errors and made many valuable story-related comments as well.

Others helped us with technical questions. Thanks to Katina Mallon for her advice on the first-aid sequence in *Child of Fire* and to Aidan Hosler for reviewing the combat sequences in *Warriors* and helping us understand the necessary demographics of seagoing trading villages.

This volume is dedicated to all these readers collectively. They will receive prize volumes, and in our telling of these times we will not forget them.

As we finish this fifth book we are working on two more, and the pace of our writing activity grows year by year. None of it would be possible without Mary and Paul. They have given their support and direct help from the start, and no relief is in sight. Our deepest thanks to both.

- JH & PH
June, 2016

Resources

THE 1991 DISCOVERY of Ötzi, the Italian/Austrian glacier mummy, is a boon to anyone interested in Neolithic culture. Excellent documentation is available on the Internet and in book form. We are particularly fortunate in that Ötzi's life was contemporary to the Benchland setting. Not only do his dress and belongings draw a remarkably clear and complete picture, but the resulting intense investigation of the region of the discovery has revealed mass graves in villages devastated by raids.

We particularly appreciate *The Man in the Ice,* the 1994 book by Konrad Spindler, the archaeologist and historian who became the mummy's lead investigator. Ötzi has been in the news again recently, as new forensic analysis reveals that he was murdered. These developments are described in a PBS documentary—see benchland.com/resources.

The authors

JAY HOSLER AND PEGGY HARRISON are professional musicians, colleagues in orchestral and chamber music for more than forty years. They began writing fiction collaboratively in 2011 and have a variety of works in progress. They previously published the first two volumes of *Norm and Burny*, a five-book series for middle readers, and the first two volumes of the *Benchland* series. *Ring of Fire* is the third and final volume.

Peggy Harrison lives with her husband, Paul, in Keller, Texas; Jay Hosler lives with his wife, Mary, in Santa Cruz, California. The two couples have been friends for decades.

Praise for Rockslide

. . . a delight to read. Better than a movie, and exactly the experience a book is meant to give. Thank you for the escape to another beautiful place and time. Can't wait for The Spirit Chamber.

. . . a book I would love to have read aloud to my fifth graders . . . I was always on the lookout for books that modeled strong, affirmative relationships among people. The cave people genuinely cared for one another and respected their diverse characters and abilities. It is good to see the women presented as strong, resourceful, and intelligent . . . pulse-racing danger. Even at my age, I was completely caught up in it.

. . . The reader is likely to be captivated by this story of the sheer will of several people thrown together by fate . . . Don't be surprised if this story tugs at the soul.

Reviews from amazon.com

Praise for Norm and Burny

"I wouldn't hesitate to recommend for advanced readers of seven and up as long as they're in good company to keep from getting too scared. By age nine, they shouldn't need to hide under the bed . . . Highly recommended."

"Good humor, exciting adventures, charming characters, and lovely illustrations."

"I curled up in bed with crackers and milk and had 2 1/2 glorious hours of regression to my childhood."

"If you love animals or have ever tried to imagine what they might be thinking, you will find this to be a quite wonderful tale . . . The Illustrations were beautiful. This book is funny & heart warming with characters you'll love . . . especially the dog."

"We just finished reading this book as one of our home school read-aloud selections. It was a Christmas gift. My daughter (11) says it is now one of her favorites. My son (9) thought it was good. We can't wait for the second book."

"The sophistication and humor are well balanced with the excitement of the adventures."

Reviews from amazon.com

If you enjoyed this book . . .

Please write a review

Your review on **amazon.com** and **goodreads.com**
will help promote the book!

Please visit Benchland.org

Buy our books!
Join our mailing list—be the first to know!
Keep in touch by liking our Facebook page.

Tell your friends
about the Benchland series
and *Ring of Fire!*